"Aleytys, I concede that you could take out any of my Hunters even without the special implants. But you're potentially dangerous for us. We're not a charitable organization. We hunt for money, not for any illusive glory. We are mercenaries, hired for specific purposes and required not to go beyond those purposes if we want to collect our fees. We do not get involved with native populations."

Aleytys let a smile tug at the corners of her mouth. "I concede the point, Head. I do get involved."

"I expect you to make a strong effort to grow out of that. Then you'll be a quite remarkable asset to Hunters, Inc." Head bundled the fax sheets together. "I've labored that point long enough. *The RMoahl are becoming troublesome. They want you. . . .*"

The Novels of the Diadem:

STAR
HUNTERS

Jo Clayton

DAW BOOKS, INC.

Donald A. Wollheim,   Publisher

1633 Broadway, New York, N.Y. 10019

FIRST PRINTING, JULY 1980

1 2 3 4 5 6 7 8 9

 DAW TRADEMARK REGISTERED
U.S. PAT. OFF. MARCA
REGISTRADA. HECHO EN U.S.A.

PRINTED IN U.S.A.

Chapter I

★ ★ ★ ★ ★ ★ ★

The faras stepped daintily through the scattered rocks and began walking along the edge of the escarpment. The Sawasawa valley floor far below stretched into the blue distance, dry and lifeless, the scattered patches of juapepo growing over it like tufts of hair on a mangy cat. Films of red dust rose, rode the wind in brief spurts, then dropped. "A long time away, Shindi." He leaned forward and scratched at the base of his mount's roached mane. The faras tossed his horned head and snorted with pleasure. Manoreh chuckled. "Run in the pastures and roll in the wet grass. We'll both be home soon." He slapped at the pouch slung over his shoulder and smiled at the rustle of the parchment inside. "With a good bit of new land mapped for the Director."

Jua Churukuu the sun was hanging low in the east. He squinted matte indigo eyes at the lime-green sun, passed a long-fingered hand over the wiry tangle of his indigo hair. In the strengthening light the faint scale markings on his silvery-green skin became a bit more prounounced. He shifted in the saddle. "Tomorrow night, Shindi," he murmured. "You'll be in your pasture and I. . . ." He grimaced. "I'll be swallowing Kobe's insults and quarreling with Kitosime."

The faras's split hooves clacked rapidly over the stone, the tidy sound tick-tocking into the soft whispering of the wind. The memory of his last encounter with his wife was still vivid in his mind even though six months had drifted by since then. *A long time,* he thought. *Too long? She wants me to take up my father's land and get away from Kobe. My father's land. . . .* Harsh, painful memories. A line of bodies stretching out, out. Endlessly. His mouth tightened. *No! Never! Let the land raise weeds and vermin.* He glanced down at the Sawasawa, closer now as the escarpments flattened and lowered toward a ripple of foothills.

5

The dust clouds seemed thicker as they hovered in a crimson haze over the brush. Manoreh frowned. Something moved down there. He halted the faras, leaning forward, straining to penetrate the haze.

Flashes of white thickened to a ragged blanket that smothered the soil and brush. Hares. A hare march. "Meme Kalamah, mother protect us," he whispered. "So many of them. I've never seen so many . . . sweeping clean this time . . . everyone . . . Ah!" He groaned. "So many . . . so many . . . so many. . . ." His hands began to shake. He saw again the bodies of his people. The watuk blindrage ignited and began to take him. He raised his head and howled.

The faras danced about, jerking his head back and forth. For a moment Manoreh's body kept balance automatically while he sank deeper into the uncontrollable rage that shook him like a rag and slammed into the FEELING centers of the faras. Then, with a high ululating whine, the animal plunged and reared, throwing him off his back to crash onto the rock. Then the faras ran blindly forward, seeking the easiest way even in his panic, leaving Manoreh stretched out on the rock, blood running sluggishly from a short cut on his head.

When Manoreh woke, the sun was shining directly into his eyes. He sat up slowly, clutched at his throbbing head. Then he remembered the hare march and grunted onto his feet. For a moment he stood swaying, eyes shut, head throbbing, then he forced himself to look at the valley. The herd was still passing, there seemed to be no end of them. He rubbed his eyes. A force weighed heavily on him, stifling, oppressive, impersonal. *Haribu,* he thought. *Driving them.* He pressed his hand to his head. *The Holders . . . have to warn them . . . Kitosime. . . .*

Manoreh stumbled away from the edge of the cliff and began walking along the faint trail. As he walked, the pounding of his boots against the stone sent flashes of light and pain stabbing into his brain. Grimly he kept on. Gradually his body settled into a comfortable long stride and the ache in his head eased to a dull throbbing that he could ignore. The feel of Haribu was oppressive but bearable since the demon's attention was focused on the hare herd. For a short while Manoreh tensed himself against a probe, but the blast of rage that had set him afoot must have been too brief to call Haribu's attention.

The barren stone gave way to sun-dried grass and red

earth. Manoreh topped a gentle rise and stopped, startled. Several lines of hares were heading for the main herd on the valley floor. He stood, clouds of red dust blowing around him, perplexed by what he was seeing. Hares traveling naturally moved a few paces forward, stopped to graze, moved on, walked a few steps on their extra-long hind legs, dropped on fours again, grazed—continuing this irregular but patterned movement throughout the day. He saw these marching like mechanical soldiers down the hillside and a shiver rippled through his body. He closed his eyes. *Hare walk . . . the line of the dead . . . no! Breathe in . . . breathe out . . . slow . . . slow . . . order straying thoughts into rhythmic patterns. The mountains call me, blue mountains eating the green sky, the plains call me, the great grass sea. . . .*

Manoreh swung into a smooth lope he could maintain for hours. As he ran, he kept the songs flowing in his mind and ignored the familiar disorientation thrown at him by the patches of juapepo as the hundreds of receptor nodes picked up his emotions and retransmitted them, mixing them with snatches of the plants' own irritations and fears, snatches of the hungers, terrors and satisfactions of every insect, reptile and rodent nesting among its roots.

Hares in the hills. None of the teaching songs spoke of hares outside the Sawasawa, even the songs of Angaleh the Wanderer, who'd mapped most of the Grass Plain in the far side of the mountains. Manoreh smiled. Angaleh the legend. Poet and singer. Explorer and mystic. Forgotten now except for his songs and the stories about him, sunk into the anonymity of the Directorship of the Tembeat. Manoreh smiled again. During the past half-year he'd added a small new triangle of territory to Angeleh's maps.

The land dipped and flattened. Manoreh slowed to a walk, the hare rumble closing in on him until he wove a precarious path through the lurching bodies of the hares ambling along at the edge of the monster herd. More than ever he regretted the loss of the faras. By nightfall he could have been. . . . He dismissed could-have-beens and lengthened his stride, closing his mind to the hares.

But he couldn't shut out memory. *Haribu Haremaster.* Manoreh's feet thudded against the ground, moving faster and faster as the sight and smell of the hares triggered the watuk blindrage, and that rage disrupted the rhythm of his breathing and the coordination of his body. He stumbled,

slowed, took in great gulps of dusty hot air . . . lost in
memories. . . .

The hare walk . . . the tide of white pouring over the
land stripping it greedily. . . .

He groaned.

The line of bodies stretching out and out . . . the days
following the line of the dead with Faiseh beside him,
burying his kin, bonded and blood . . . bodies . . . father . . . mother . . . sister. . . .

He sobbed. Tears cut through the mask of dust on his face.

His sister splashed out on the ground clutching her dead
baby, arms and legs twitching, eyes blank, face empty,
every touch of human burned out of her. . . .

He tried to hold her, slapped her, tried to wake her out of
that terrible blank animal state. There was nothing left in her.
He knelt beside her, watched her for awhile. Faiseh found
him there, offered to do what was necessary, but Manoreh
shook his head. As the moonring became visible in the darkening sky, he pressed his fingers against her throat and waited
until the artery was still under his fingers. He buried her, the
baby on her breast, and went on with Faiseh until there were
no more twitching bodies.

Hare walk. Driven to walk and walk. To walk without
stopping. To walk until muscles no longer responded to
will. To crawl. Finally to lie on the ground, hands and
feet twitching while the last feeble glow of life dimmed
and died.

He groaned as he thought of the hares ringing Kobe's Holding, focusing their malice on the Kisima clan . . . on Kitosime . . . on his son Hodarzu . . . until minds burned out
and they began to walk.

Manoreh's foot caught under a juapepo root and he
crashed heavily into the red dust. The pain jarred him out of
his memories. He pushed onto his knees as the juapepo
picked up and reinforced his pain. He sucked in a deep

breath and began pulling together the Tembeat discipline, distancing himself from the troubling emotion, slowing the body, filling the mind. He got clumsily to his feet and looked up. Jua Churukuu was halfway down the western arc of his day path. He turned and faced along his backtrail. The grumble of the hares was a low murmur on the horizon. Around him scattered herds of kudu leaped and galloped to the northeast, frantic to get away from the creeping menace behind them. He checked the urge to race with them. If his spurt of blindrage had exhausted him, it had at least won him a long lead on the hare herd. Enough. No good burning himself out. The warning had to be given. He swung back into the lope, his body moving smoothly, the thick red dust stirring about his feet.

An hour later he stopped to rest a few moments at a water tree standing in the middle of a mud slick. He knelt by the multiple trunks and drank from the small cold stream, heard a rustling in the coarse grass growing rankly about the slick. A hare pushed out of the grass and sat daintily at the edge of the mud, bulging brown eyes staring blankly at him. Another rustle and a second hare crouched beside the first. *The blindrage*, he thought ruefully. *This time Haribu noticed it.* The hares rubbed the sides of their heads together, then rose onto their hind legs, eyes fixed on him, long ears pointing stiffly at him. He felt a dulling pressure. His sight blurred. There was a whining in his ears.

Working against a compulsion strong as tangleweb, he forced his hand to the darter on his belt.

The hares' noses twitched and the pressure on him increased. His hand inched down, unsnapped the holster flap, eased the pistol out. The hares shook and whined. The pressure built higher. He emptied the magazine into the hares, the darts phutting into the white fur or skimming past into the grass behind. He staggered as the pressure was suddenly cut off.

The grass stirred again. He wheeled to face the new danger, frightened and angry.

A wilding boy stood watching him. He was small and wiry, his green-silver skin stained and dirty. He watched to see what Manoreh would do, then projected a complex FEELING: QUESTION?/DESIRE.

Manoreh holstered the darter. "Who are you?" he asked,

hoping for but not expecting an answer. Wildings never spoke.

The boy waited, still sending his silent message.

Manoreh sighed and projected: QUESTION?

The boy smiled, his dark blue eyes laughing. He pointed to the dead hares. QUESTION?

Manoreh nodded. Projected: ASSENT.

The wilding boy scooped up the hare bodies. Trailing a broad APPRECIATION, he trotted off and was lost in the haze of dust.

The sun dipped lower and the cloud cover spread a growing shadow over the Sawasawa. Manoreh ran steadily, his feet beating to the rhythm of the bush songs he repeated continuously to ward off the betraying memories.

He heard the hounds before he saw the Fa-men coming toward him. He stopped, mouth pressed into a grim line as the red-eyed dogs circled around him, growling and snapping at his boots, yellow teeth clicking together a hair away from the leather. Fa-men. There was a sickness in his stomach when he thought of them. Dangerous fanatics. Hating the wildings and everything to do with the Wild. Hating all products of technology which they called corrupting abominations. They wore animal furs, despising woven cloth. They carried assegais rather than darters or pellet rifles and were expert in their use. He was in some danger, he knew that. They tolerated the Tembeat but that toleration was easily strained. They cultivated the blindrage and gloried in the bloody results.

The Fa-men rode slowly toward him, their hatred reaching him, sickening him yet more until he was at the point of vomiting. There were four of them, assegais at ready. Ignoring the hounds, they spread out and stopped their mounts so that all were facing him, spear points less than a meter away.

"Wild Ranger." The Fa-kichwa stroked the scars on his right cheek then jabbed his assegai at Manoreh. "Trying out the wilding boys?"

The Sniffer giggled shrilly. "Sold four legs for a two-leg ride." Sniffer jabbed at him, the spear point drawing blood from his arm just below the shoulder. "What'd you do with your faras, little Ranger? Huh? Huh! HUH!" He was a little man, twisted and so ugly that the yellow river clay painted on his skin and the black-worked scars on his face disappeared before his monumental hideousness, a meager man, skin stretched taut over tiny bones. He continued to poke at

Manoreh, working himself into a dangerous state of excitement.

"Mohj-sniff!" The kichwa's voice was indulgent but firm. "Back off. You—Wild Ranger." The sneer in the words was deliberately exaggerated. "Your clan? What are you doing here?"

"Clan Hazru, Mezee Fa-Kichwa. Took the harewalk three years ago. I affiliate with Kobe of Kisima, being wed to his daughter." His voice was low and uncertain. He knew they relished his weakness and this angered him. But the sudden caution that damped their hate when they heard his father-in-law's name gave him a small, bitter satisfaction. He sucked in a deep breath. "The hares march, Fa-Kichwa." He shrugged. "My faras went berserk and threw me. I run now to warn the Holdings." With an outward calm he pointed the way he'd come. "Little more than three hours behind me."

"Fa!" The Fa-Kichwa looped the assegai's thong over his shoulder and wheeled his mount. By the time Manoreh faced around again, the four were galloping with their hounds toward the mountains.

He started running again, smiling at the Fa-men's panic. "Scrambling for the Standing Stones," he murmured. "Going to crouch there shivering in their boots, praying that Fa will chase the hares away."

In the thickening twilight he came to the bridge his grandfather had built across the Chumquivir, a tributary of the Mungivir which was the great river running the length of the Sawasawa. This was the southern boundary of his father's land, his now. Though several planks of the bridge were broken or missing, the pilings seemed sturdy enough. He stepped cautiously onto it, keeping close to the shaky rail. The bridge trembled underfoot and groaned each time he put pressure on it, but held him while he crossed. He stepped reluctantly into the shadow of the ufagiosh trees and walked with increasing slowness toward the place where the ufagiosh merged with a ragged emwilea hedge. The sickness in his stomach returned. His emwilea. Rank now, and wild. Canes growing haphazardly out from the tight center, coiling like poison-tipped barbed wire across the rutted earth. The high roots were choked by the round, fuzzy leaves of hareweed. When he saw a boy, a small silver-green wiggler who preferred running with the farash to grubbing in the earth, he'd spent hour after tedious hour grooming the hedge along this section of path.

He hesitated, looked up. Through the sparse leaves of the ufagio he could see the clouds lowering, as the wind whipped up the dust and the dry storm came toward him. He cursed softly. *Another plan rotted out.* He scowled toward the south. *Four hours lead on them. But the storm would slow them down some.* He walked slowly along beside the emwilea hedge, shoulders hunched over, head drawn down. Anger: hot, ready to explode and spew the pieces of his soul across the land. Grief: like acid eating at him, an itch that had no anodyne. Fear: colder than the glacial ice he'd walked the faras over when he crossed the Jinolimas coming and going. Anger-grief-fear were pressing against his consciousness.

The uauawimbony tree outside the gate postponed his anguish and rattled a warning. *No one left to warn.* Manoreh ducked under the umbrella spread of the whippy branches and rested his palm against the brain node, a dark bulge like a head sitting on a spread of twenty-four legs, the cone-shaped circle of trunks that met in the middle forming a dark secret cavity where he used to sit giggling while the wimbony whipped about like a wild thing. The tight wood was cool and soothing under his hand, reminding him of a happier time. He stood a moment reluctant to think of the painful *now*, but sand was beginning to blow, skipping like fleas under the branch tips. He ducked back under the fringe and walked to the gate.

The carved gate was knocked flat, the gateposts standing like broken teeth. The watchtower was a wreck, twisted over, spread along the ground by one of the windstorms that had blown by since he left. He knelt by the rotting gate and tore a section free. His fingers twisted in the spongy remains eaten away by time and the tunneling siafu. The wood turned to dust and splinters in his hands, and scores of siafu eggs fell onto the patchy gravel beneath. Dust. Manoreh opened his fingers and stared at the dull gray dust filming his skin. He wiped his hand across the front of his jerkin. Dust. He stood and crunched across the wood into the silent shattered quarters of the bound families. Mud houses melted away, thatching scattered and rotting, rafters jutting up like old bones. And silent. Except for the dust grains whispering along the earth and the howling wind. He walked along the rutted street, remembering the loud cries of the weavers and dyers, the clangs from the smithy, the chant of the story teller in the center of a ring of children, the shouts of children running naked through streets and side alleys. Filled with lively human voices and the noises of energetic living before the hares came, it was a silent accusation to him now. Why was he alive? And why did he leave the land dead?

The wind was rising to a howl, tugging at his tangled bush of dark blue hair. He walked silently past the emptiness, dry weeds crackling under his boots, leaves and dry weeds rolling past him, driven by the dust-laden wind that scoured at his skin and brought tears. His inner eyelids oozed upwards, triggered by the smarting and he saw less clearly, the wet transparency blocking off some of the feeble twilight. Thunder rumbled repeatedly, directly overhead as the dry storm took hold of the abandoned Holding.

He felt Haribu Haremaster tickling at him, insinuating spirit fingers into the private places of his mind. When he tried to fight free of them, he was distracted by the rage-grief-fear that walked with him into this devastation of his childhood. He pressed his hands to his face and tried to repress the boiling emotions that weakened him and pointed him out to Haribu.

It walked by his side, not touching him, a red ghost in the haze of red dust. He burned his head slowly, then bowed to the presence. The spiky head, beaked like a heraldic bird, nodded back. He walked past the court wall. Then at the archway he hesitated, wondering if the Mother Well had been covered or was choked. For a brief moment it seemed important that he know, then feeling empty, he plodded away, the red ghost matching him stride for stride. He reached the wall that enclosed the kitchen garden. The path was choked with old leaves and branches. His feet crunched through them with heavy slow regularity. His head ached. He would have wept but could not with his inner eyelids in place. He cupped his hand over his mouth and breathed deeply, a long shuddering sigh. The red presence swirled closer, wrapped its arms around him, sinking claws deep into his body, the hook beak driving toward his neck. He felt again the cold agony of his grief and the lava heat of his anger as the ghost began to merge with him.

Haribu Haremaster moved closer.

"No!" He gasped then ground his teeth together, the dust gritting, rasping at his nerves. Weighted down by the clinging specter, Haribu sniping at him, Manoreh stumbled around the corner, staggering stiff-legged through wind debris that swirled around his feet and rose in choking whorls to attack his face and hands. He shielded his face and lurched along the walkway that led to the barn.

His feet knew the stones, though everything was swallowed by darkness and dust. The red ghost slid away, but glided beside him, its dark eye smudges fixed on him. Waiting. Like Haribu waited.

Manoreh slammed into a wall. The barn. He felt along the rough bricks until he found the sliding door into the milking section. Head tucked down, holding his breath, he rocked the door loose and slid it open. He thrust himself through the narrow opening, losing some skin to the rough brick. He shouldered the door shut and turned to face the thick blackness inside.

Hands guided by old habit, he felt along the wall till he touched the lamp. Praying that after three years the wick was intact enough to take a spark, he wound it up about an inch, relaxing at the smell of the lamp oil. After a few futile attempts with the striking box, the wick caught and diluted the darkness inside the barn with a weak yellow light. The rough wooden stanchions came out of the blackness like narrow gray shadows; beyond them he saw the red ghost watching.

Ignoring it, he slapped at his leather jerkin and shorts, releasing clouds of dust. His ancestor had built well. The barn was tight against the storm. Still ignoring the ghost, he worked through the triangular gap of one of the stanchions, barely fitting where as a boy he had wriggled through with room to spare. He groped through darkness toward the back of the barn, stumbling over abandoned tools and equipment, working his way carefully toward the old wellhouse and its ancient hand pump.

As Manoreh touched the handle, worn smooth by long use, his grandfather's spirit stood beside him, a big knotted old man, dark blue laughter in his squinting eyes. Manoreh worked the handle until he heard the clean splash of water hitting the stone of the trough. This ghost, his grandfather's spirit, was a friendly, happy presence, giving Manoreh strength to fight off his aches. He plunged his hands into the cool liquid and splashed it over his face, washing away the dense coating of dust. He pumped more water and drank, swallowing again and again, feeling half his anguish vanish with his thirst.

He moved cautiously back into the fringes of light. He

could hear the silken whisper of dust driving against the barn. The storm was building. He thought of the hares crouching on the Sawasawa and smiled grimly. Hundreds of them would be dead before morning and more would be weakened, delaying their march.

He stretched and yawned, feeling comfortably tired, the spirit of his grandfather strong on him. He went to the milking lanes and brought the lamp back. Then looked around for a place to sleep. The hay was damp and stinking of mildew. Manoreh grimaced. Another indictment of his neglect. His father would be grieved. Manoreh stood quiet in the darkness hoping that Father Ancestor would come like Grandfather Ancestor, bringing peace at last and a gentler end to grieving. He did not come.

Manoreh sighed and stretched out on the floor. A hard bed and a cold one. Briefly he regretted the pack tied behind Shindi's saddle, then composed himself to sleep. Futile to regret what couldn't be helped. The lamp light wavered as the oil supply burned away. He wrinkled his nose at his lack of thought. *Open flame inside a hayfilled barn. Stupid.* He extinguished the flame then lay back staring up into the darkness.

Overhead the dry storm turned to wet and rain began to patter on the roof. He listened for leaks and felt a brief flash of pride when he heard none. He turned on his side and contemplated the bird-headed ghost crouched in the darkness, visible like an after-image against the sooty background. "I see you, ghost."

The spiky head bowed.

"Be patient, old ghost. I need you. I'll be back."

The eye smudges flickered.

"You'll wait here for me?"

The head bowed again.

"Yes, you'll wait." Manoreh winced, aware of the danger of this splitting. As time passed the ghost would begin to fade. When there was nothing left, that part of him would be gone. He would grow cold, stiff, would end as a man, even though his body continued walking around. But Haribu Haremaster was too strong. The ghost would have to stay until the Holdings were warned. And Kiwanji. He wondered vaguely if Faiseh had seen the march and was warning his own people. He drifted into an uneasy sleep.

The blackness merged to dream . . . a pale woman with skin like sick amber . . . eyes wide with surprise . . . eyes

bright blue-green like the sky at its zenith just before night
. . . a face he'd never seen before . . . a type he'd never
seen before . . . everything wrong about her for beauty . . .
shapes subtly wrong . . . texture wrong . . . lips too thin
. . . eyes wrong . . . wrong . . . too strong . . . too hard
. . . red hair . . . demon hair . . . demon color . . . probing
at him . . . projecting: QUESTION: YOU/WHO ARE YOU? WHAT
ARE YOU? . . . unafraid . . . with a forwardness he found
hard to accept in a woman . . . who are you? . . . he tried
to pull away from her . . . uncomfortable . . . disturbed by
her . . . she was magnificent . . . and wrong . . . all wrong
. . . something in him reached out to her . . . distantly he
felt her surprise . . . felt a friendly outreach and a driving
curiosity . . . he jerked away and was deep asleep in
minutes.

Chapter II

★ ★ ★ ★ ★ ★ ★

Kitosime walked down the steps, back straight, head high, swaying gracefully. After years of rigid training, her body knew its business even when her legs felt weak and her hands shook as she slid them down the railing. The courtyard was momentarily empty as was the porch behind her. The silence was cool on her skin. At the last step she stumbled but caught herself, clutching desperately at the railing. She stood shaking a moment, eyes closed, caught in a flood of terror. One flaw in her and Old Man Kobe would throw her away like a broken pot. He tolerated no spots on his prizes. She sucked in a deep breath and tried to still the shaking that held her prisoner on that step. Her favored status was her son's safety. *Hodarzu, ah Meme Kalamah, why did he have to be like his father . . . and me . . . ah . . . me . . . me . . . me.* She glanced over her shoulder at the heavy throne chair blocking the way to the main door. Kobe liked to look at her. He kept her kneeling beside him when he sat in that chair, her back straight, her neck straight, her head held proudly. A living ornament, a testimony to his wealth and power as he made his ponderous judgments. Kitosime the favorite daughter. Kitosime the beautiful. Kitosime the elegant, the perfect expression of the power of his blood.

She shivered and stepped carefully onto the painted tiles of the courtyard. Grateful for the brief solitude, a rare gift, she walked slowly to the Mother Well in the center of the enclosed space. *I can't endure it,* she thought. *I drown. I am empty.* She rested one hand on the well coping and tilted her head to look at the heavy red clouds that were garish against the morning sky's bright yellow green, remnants of last night's twin storms. Not much time left for her. Kobe would be out in a little while and expect to find her waiting.

17

The tiles gritted under her sandals as she shifted from foot
to foot beside the great well. Though the day was already
hot, coolness touched her face. "Meme Kalamah," she whispered. "Surround my son, hide him. Give me strength to endure, great Mother." The well whispered back to her, a low
liquid murmur that steadied her. "Help me." The returning
whisper was soft and confiding. She felt the coolness bathing
her, smoothing away her weakness. She turned away, then
stopped with a soft exclamation; something had bruised her
foot through the thin leather of her sandal sole. She knelt.

Two small stones huddled next to the well, dull gray
pebbles with holes like eyes in the centers. "Eyestones," she
whispered. She lifted them carefully and placed them on her
hennaed palm. They lay on her painted skin, cold and com-
plete with power, taking nothing from the warmth of her
body. Slowly she opened the pouch that hung on a leather
thong about her neck and eased the stones inside. Filled with
a sense of terrifying portent, she glided from the courtyard
wanting to run but not able to. She was Bighouse and
Bighouse didn't run. Ever.

In the quarter the bound families were hard at work. She
walked through the cheerful din like a dark ghost, ignored
and unable to join in. In the spinners' circle the women were
chatting and laughing, teasing a young bride, sitting
crosslegged about a basket of fleece, fingers busy shaping the
thread, rolling it on hard knees, winding it on the spindles.
Several of the women had their babies with them, sleeping
comfortably in the long cloth slings that bound them tight
against their mothers' backs. From time to time the women
broke into a work chant while the spindles danced and
twirled.

They fell silent as she passed. She could feel their eyes following her. They knew what she'd come for. They know everything, those women. She envied them their freedom. They
could move and laugh without constraint, they could make
awkward gestures without losing what was more than life to
them. She touched her hair. It was a measure of the distance
between her and these her sisters. Plaited into elaborate coils,
it took two women an hour each morning to fashion what
was really a miniature sculpture.

She passed blacksmith and tinsmith beating against their
metal, the metal crying back in deep ringing protest. She

passed the potter kicking his wheel while his sons beat the air from piles of reluctant clay. She passed women holding stone bowls between their knees, grinding agazu root to paste for the many-layered honey pastry. Passed others preparing dyes, or stirring sodden cloth in great cauldrons, the sweat forming rivers on their faces and bodies. She envied them their sweat. The noise died away before her and swelled behind. She walked with the grace of Kobe's favored daughter, and wanted to groan and cry out her torment, wanted to laugh and work, even to sweat. Instead she went to Papa Goh's odorus hut for the fezza seed that dulled her senses and made her life possible.

She halted in front of the isolated hutch painted a dull black and scrawled over with cryptic symbols written in white river clay. Her hands were shaking again. Remembering her training, she tapped her fingers lightly against the skin of the small drum.

It was hotter inside than by the dryers' fires. By some trick of construction the hut caught the sun and trapped its heat under the mud-plastered thatch. Heat shimmered around the skinny naked figure of a tiny man. His eyes were closed into slits and his skin was tarnished like old silver; he was almost lost among the shadows. Kitosime suppressed a gasp as she sank onto her knees and drew in a breath of the fetid atmosphere compounded of urine and ancient sweat, of death and a thousand different drugs.

She waited, hands on her thighs, palms up, fingers curving into flower petals, a silent begging which was all her pride allowed her.

Papa Goh shifted irritably. "Are the bones to speak? You want to know where your man wanders instead of staying home and plowing your field?" He cackled maliciously, then stopped as her face kept its doll mask. "You waste my time, woman."

"Fezza seed," she said. Her voice was a doll's voice, musical but lifeless. She touched the pouch hanging around her neck, fighting back anger. He knew very well what she wanted but relished his small triumphs over her. Slowly she pulled the pouch open and reached inside. She hesitated as her fingers touched the eyestones, then dug further for the cool slickness of metal. He watched avidly as she pulled out a large copper coin and placed it on the floor in front of him.

"Not enough. Not enough." Flecks of spittle sprayed out from his toothless mouth. One landed on the back of her hand. She wanted to scrub the hand against the dirt, wanted to scramble to her feet and tear her way out of the stinking darkness. Instead she brushed lightly at the moisture then fished out a second coin and placed it beside the first. She waited, hands resting lightly on her thighs.

Papa Goh snorted and scooped up the coins, then he took a bit of crumpled paper, twisted it into a cone and scooped a handful of dark brown seeds into the top. He thrust the screw of paper at her.

Kitosime took the seeds, repressing a shudder at having to touch his fingers and take the wretched paper. But she smiled, murmured the proper farewells and dipped out the low door.

She stood blinking in the morning sunlight, drawing in great gulps of air to flush the foulness out of her system. Then the gong sounded, Kobe would be coming out. Expecting her to be waiting. She fumbled in the twist of paper and thrust three of the seeds into her mouth. The others she stuffed hastily into the neck pouch. Her heart juddered in her breast and the veins at her temples throbbed. She pressed her hands against her eyes and bit down on the seeds in her mouth, letting the juice slide down her parched throat. There was a frantic clacking in her ears. She shuddered. Then the true meaning of the noise reached her and she looked around.

The uauawimbony tree was jerking about, the seed pods rattling loudly. Kitosime tightened the roll knot over her breasts, reset the brooch pin and smoothed the dress cloth along her sides. She knew who the watch-tree announced. *Manoreh's back,* she thought. *Why?*

The watchman leaning out from his tower echoed her question unknowingly. "Well, Badnews," he roared down, "is this official or are you coming to visit your wife at last?"

Kitosime winced. All the world knew the privacies of her marriage. Briefly she hated Manoreh for subjecting her to this. But the fezza was beginning to work; she drifted along the road letting the noise flow over her without really hearing it. Only the shouted words at the gate reached her.

"I have business with Old Man Kobe, Watcher. Let me through."

She heard the clink of the gate bar as she turned the cor-

ner and floated toward the arch that led into the courtyard.
Something was wrong. She considered the situation coolly.
Hare march. Why else ask for Kobe? She felt a distant thrill
of fear which she knew would be terror without the fezza.
There was danger in this for her son. Not from the hares, no,
from his kin. . . . If she were locked in with them for days
and days, locked in with Kobe and his fanatic hatred of the
wildings, locked in until Hodarzu betrayed himself, until she
cracked wide and betrayed her own smothered but still
present ability to FEEL. The terror grew, in spite of the fezza.
She stopped by the well. Kobe was not out yet, thank the
good Mother. She leaned heavily against the coping. "Meme
Kalamah, help me," she whispered. She fumbled in the neck-
pouch and fished out two more seeds. With the juice blunting
her fear, she watched, distantly amused, as Kobe came out of
the house, followed by a stream of servants, one carrying the
kneeling cushion, another the table that stood at Kobe's elbow, a third, Kobe's beer mug and the tall pitcher of Minimi's brew, a fourth, the special cushion he sat on, and a
humble fifth, cloths to dust the throne chair.

Kitosime left the well and drifted toward him, like a
prisoned but unconcerned goldfish swimming in cool water
that kept the hate and fear outside the glass. She giggled behind her doll mask, a silent spiteful giggle as she walked with
deliberately exaggerated grace across the painted tiles and up
the stairs under his appreciative eyes. She knelt on the cushion, straightened her back, lifted her head, and smiled her
doll's smile at the Kisimash pouring into the courtyard following Manoreh, silent worried people waiting for news they
didn't want to hear.

He looks odd, she thought. *Tired. But more than that.* She
felt the pricking of curiosity but the fezza took away her
will. *He's been long away at a time I needed him.* The fezza
washed above the anger, damping down its fumes, sparking
only a flow of thought passing behind her doll's face. . . .

Hodarzu feels, Manoreh, and Kobe will give him to the
Fa-men, and they will roast and eat him, my little son.
As he'll throw you, Manoreh, my husband.
As soon as he's sure he doesn't need you to take pos-
session of your land, all of it, unshared by other council
members.

At one stroke he doubles his land and his power, Manoreh.

And he hates you, Manoreh.

Even through the fezza dullness it sickens me, his hate.

He can claim the land through Hodarzu too, Manoreh,
so be careful, my husband, you walk on a thread that
could break any minute, Manoreh.

Once the Fa-men have you, Manoreh, what happens to
me?

He hates the wildings, Manoreh, he goes to the Fa-men's
burnings and eats the burned flesh.

He has a taste for wilding flesh.

See how hungrily he eyes you, Manoreh; he marks your
flesh for a meal.

Soon, I think, he'll have you.

And when he has the land in those tiny, greedy hands,
Manoreh, he'll eat my son.

The words unreeled before her eyes, tangible things. She
sat with her head high, face empty so expression would not
mar its pure beauty. A possession of the Old Man, Kobe of
Kisima clan, her father who would throw her to the scav-
engers if he suspected what she needed the fezza seed to hide.

Manoreh stood quietly at the foot of the stairs, waiting for
Kobe to acknowledge his presence. His eyes rested briefly on
her but he said nothing to her, turning back to Kobe as if
something like fezza fulled his reactions also.

"Wild Ranger," Kobe said heavily.

Manoreh bowed his head politely, then he fixed calm eyes
on Kobe. "Kobe ya Kimbizi aya Fajir iya Fundi iyai Kisima,
the hares march." He paused, waiting for questions that
didn't come. "They follow about three hours, perhaps four,
behind me, a herd so wide it blankets the Sawasawa." His
shoulders slumped briefly before he straightened them, stubbornly refusing to show weakness in the face of Kobe's hostility. Kitosime was vaguely worried. *He's terribly tired, Meme
Kalamah keep him. . . .* She breathed in the mist of hate
and fear directed toward him. *Manoreh, Manoreh why do
you try to endure this? Take up your father's land and get us
both away. Why, why, why don't you do that?*

"Kiwanji." Kobe grimaced; his eyes opened wide until
rings of white showed around the indigo. Kitosime rocked
slightly on the kneeling pillow, struggling to maintain her

mask. *Meme Kalamah, help me, help me. I can't stand it. The hate, the hate. . . .*

"The psi-screens will keep the people safe." Manoreh's face froze. After a minute he said hoarsely, "You haven't seen what happens in a hare walk. Make up your mind, Old Man."

"Psi-screens. Abomination." Kobe twisted small hands on the elaborately carved chair arms. "No!" He scowled at the line of blue where the eastern mountain crests rippled above the court walls. "The mountains will hold us. The Fa-shrine."

Kitosime jerked, almost cried out. As she calmed herself she saw Manoreh's face freeze over again. He was silent for a long moment, then said quietly, "If these were all young men—" he moved his hands in a quick circle, taking in all the folk in the courtyard—"used to hard riding and hard living, you might make it." His mouth snapped shut. She felt the coldness in him. His eyes rested on her. "If you go to the mountains," he said tautly, "I want my wife and son. I've lost enough close kin to the hares."

"Hold your noise!" Kobe snapped. Kitosime swayed again, fighting to cope with a tiny spark of hope. *To get out of here, ride with Manoreh, get Hodarzu someplace safe. . . .* She swayed back and forth rhythmically, blanking out both hope and fear, but deep within, the chant was softly repeated: *Talk to me, Manoreh, just one minute, take a minute and talk to me, I'm your wife, talk to me. . . .* She fixed her eyes on him silently begging him to use his FEELING and hear her need.

"I've got no choice," Kobe said sourly. "We'll take the barges into Kiwanji." His little dark eyes glittered. "No need to take my daughter scrambling through the wild." His tiny hands closed into fists. *He won't let me go*, Kitosime thought dully. *Even if Manoreh bothered to try, he'd stop him somehow. And he won't try. . . .*

Manoreh's eyes flicked to Kitosime then dismissed her. "Give me a faras, Old Man. And let me go. The other Holders still aren't warned of the hare march."

Kobe grunted. *He wants to refuse*, Kitosime thought. *But he doesn't dare.* The Old Man rose. "So," he said, "go to the corral and pick your own." He stumped back into the house, trailed by the silent house servants.

"Manoreh." Kotosime called to her husband, but he was pushing his way through the murmuring, hostile crowd filling

the courtyard and didn't hear her. Kneeling gracefully erect
on her pillow, afraid to call him again, she watched him dis-
appear through the arch. As the silent crowd began trickling
out behind him, she rose and walked slowly into the house. *I
wish I knew what to do, where to go . . .*

Chapter III

★ ★ ★ ★ ★ ★ ★

The uauawimbony tree clattered as Manoreh rode out, and the dance of the faras's hooves rattling against the gold-brown gravel echoed the sound. Manoreh loosened the reins a little, letting the faras move into a trot, thinking unhappily about Kitosime. He had a vague sense of foreboding but couldn't track down any cause for it. He tried to shake it off. *I should have taken a minute to talk to her.* He grimaced. *Women!*

He pushed the faras hard along the rutted road that ran beside the Mungivir. The wind was rising again, sending dust skittering through the juapepo. Overhead the clouds thickened across the sun's face, casting a shadow over the land. The haze of red dust whirled about him, reminding him of the dream woman's long fine hair. Abruptly he could feel her looking at him. She was getting closer and closer. He tried to concentrate on the ride.

Aleytys narrowed her eyes as the face ghosting across the stars was abruptly gone, the face that invaded her dreams and continued to puzzle her. She leaned back and watched Grey, silent in the pilot seat. He felt her looking, smiled at her, then went back to the tapes detailing the Hunt. *My Hunt,* she thought. She rubbed her fingertips along the chair arms. *First of many. Until I earn a ship. A ship of my own....* She closed her eyes. *My Hunt.*

Head turned from the window. She was a chunky, middle-aged woman with stiff silver hair worn short like a cap. Her smile flashed wide, white, brilliant. "University sends me good reports of your progress."

Aleytys smoothed the material over her thighs. "That's encouraging."

25

"It seems you've also followed instructions and kept quiet about your background and your . . . um . . . talents." Head charged at the desk and got her body into a chair without kicking it over. "Good." She leaned back, heavy eyebrows rising.

Aleytys told herself there was no reason to be nervous. Even if Head had sent a special ship to University to fetch her. She smiled uncertainly. "That's no occasion for praise. Living is easier when the people around me don't treat me like a freak."

"No doubt." Head placed a pile of fax sheets in front of her. "We've expended a lot of credit on you. One way or another." She paused and looked down at the sheets. "And protected you from some powerful enemies."

Aleytys looked down. "I'm aware of that."

"Um." Head leafed through the fax sheets, pulled out one and read it while Aleytys watched, swallowing the knot in her throat. After a moment Head flattened her hand on the sheet and looked up at her. "You've made no friends. A year ago you quarreled with Grey and he walked out on you. Since then you've been withdrawing from human contact until you hardly bother to leave your rooms except for classes. Would you care to explain?"

"No."

"What?" Head frowned.

"I think I was clear. How I prefer to live is my business."

Head settled back in her chair, her shrewd eyes moving from Aleytys's face to the hands curled into fists. "Sore point?" Her pale blue eyes rose to Aleytys's face again. "Anything that might affect your performance is my business. I don't want to think I made a bad decision when I admitted you to training." When Aleytys remained stubbornly silent, she continued. "Part of what we sell is our reputation, mountain girl. I repeat. Why?"

Aleytys slid her tongue over her lips. "I'm more comfortable by myself."

Head's fingers tapped on the sheets. "If you were Wolff-born . . . Part Vryhh, part god knows. . . ." She sighed. "There's more to this. What's bothering you?"

Aleytys closed her eyes. "All right. I have problems relating to people. According to the letter my mother left when she abandoned me, the Vrya all find it difficult to maintain close personal relationships."

Head looked skeptical. "You weren't maintaining any relationships at all."

"So?"

The chunky woman fixed her eyes on Aleytys until she started to fidget. After several minutes of this uncomfortable silence, she said, "You don't take orders very well, do you?"

Aleytys moved impatiently. "I don't see the point of all this. Why bring me from University just to dig at me?"

"If I sent you out on a Hunt. . . ." Her eyes twinkled as Aleytys forced back the words that wanted to pour out. "You've been given access to classified material concerning a Hunter's biologic implants?"

Aleytys nodded.

"Um. I'd planned to schedule for surgery at the end of this year. You'd have spent the next year learning how to use them."

"Had planned?"

"Keep still and listen. You aren't ready to Hunt. And don't give me any argument about that. I concede that you could take out any of my Hunters even without the implants. But you're politically naïve and potentially disastrous for us. Special skills aside, you've got a lot to learn, young woman. Among other things, the limitations to our commissions. We're not a charitable organization. We can't afford to be. Wolff is a poor world. We hunt for money, Aleytys. Not for any illusive glory. Not from any moral imperative. We are mercenaries, hired for specific purposes and required not to go beyond those purposes if we want to collect our fees."

Aleytys brushed impatiently at her hair. "I know that."

"I don't think you do." Head's lips tightened as she searched Aleytys's face. "We do not—cannot—get involved with native populations."

Aleytys lifted a hand, let it drop. A smile started. "I concede the point. I do get involved."

"So you do. As I said, potentially disastrous for us."

"You knew that before you sent me to University."

"Of course. I expect you to make a strong effort to grow out of that sentimentality, mountain girl. Then you'll be a quite remarkable asset to Hunters Inc." Head bundled the fax sheets together, extracted a ragged slip of paper, then dropped them into the destructor. "I've labored that point long enough. The RMoahl are becoming troublesome. They want you."

"You said you'd talk them out of harassing me."

"Hard-headed bastards. Unreasonable." She wrinkled her beaky nose. "They're still determined to lock you up in their treasure vault until you die so they can get their diadem back."

"Their diadem, hah!"

"It has been in their hands for several thousand years. A reasonable claim to ownership." Head shrugged. "Fortunately they have an exaggerated respect for authority. University is a neutral world and they are unable because of their culture to violate that neutrality, so we have no problem as long as you stay there."

"Yet you called me here."

"Yes."

"I see." Aleytys smiled. "You've decided to use me in spite of my potential for disaster."

"Um." Head looked a little uncomfortable, then picked up the small scrap of paper. "Someone's heard about you."

"What?"

Head frowned at the scrawled words on the paper. "We've had a Hunt proposed. Chwereva Company. A world called Sunguralingu."

"So?"

"The Reps made a condition. That you be assigned to the Hunt."

"That smells."

"Very ripe. Your talents are tailored for this Hunt but how the hell could they know about you?"

Aleytys stared blankly at the window behind Head. "I've banged up against several companies," she said slowly. "The Karkesh on Lamarchos, though I don't see . . . they knew me only as a native sorceress. Ffynch Company on Irsud. The Rep there was poking about, looked like the type that could ferret out anything he wanted to know. Wei-chu-Hsien on Maeve. Their present Rep there saw a lot more than I feel comfortable about. But you know that. I'm sure you read Grey's report."

Head nodded. "It's not impossible, it just stinks. I decided to refuse the Hunt."

"Then why am I here?"

"As you said, a bad smell about the whole thing. I opened my mouth to refuse. And changed my mind."

"Why?"

"Good question." Head's eyes were hard and angry. "I intended to tell the Rep it was not possible but before the words came out they changed on me."

"Ah! I see." Aleytys frowned. "But your shield. . . ."

"Tell me about it." Head shook her head. "I can't prove coercion so we're stuck with the Hunt. Find out how I was reached in spite of the defenses of this office. And my own personal defenses. Do the best you can with Chwereva's problem, but find out for me how that bastard got to me."

Aleytys rubbed thumb and forefinger together. "I could, I think. Reach you, I mean. But a competent brain scan would show my tampering. Did you . . . no, that's stupid, of course you did. What did it show?"

"Not much."

"The Reps. What did they look like?"

"Hardly your typical watuk. Talker was sloppy fat. Important syb of one of the Eight Families on Watulkingu. Director in Chwereva. Had a twirp with him. Paper carrier, negligible as far as I could tell. Couldn't make an impression on a milk pudding if he sat on it. Third one was interesting. Watuk features, coloring, scale markings. Tall man, grotesquely thin, wearing an exoskeleton." Head raised a hand as Aleytys looked up. "No. Analyzed before he got in here. Exoskeleton and nothing else. Very nice drivers. Take a look at schematics when you go through the files. Serd-amachar syndrome. Why he wore it. Wasting disease with no known cure. Under his clothes he was bone and a bit of dried-out skin."

"Maybe the RMoahl?"

"No. Not their style."

"Then a psi-freak like me. One of those three."

"No point in pooling ignorance. Since this is your first Hunt proposal, I have to explain that you may turn it down if you choose. That would let us off the hook. I hope you don't. However, before you decide, you should know this. You won't go out alone this time. I'm going to link you to another Hunter. We'll take time for one of the implants. A minor operation. Just to set in a tracer. I want you to have a backup. Hunters Inc. itself is riding on this."

"Who's going with me?"

"Grey."

"What! No, I can't. . . ."

Head watched her quietly. "Grey has seen you work. And

he's a professional. And he knows you. He can head you off if you start running wild. Whatever stands between you, he won't let it interfere with the Hunt." Her strong face turned stern. "Make no mistake, Aleytys. He's in charge. Do what he tells you. Blow this Hunt and we drop you, never mind what we've spent on you."

"Do what he tells me." Aleytys scowled. "Even if I think he's got rats in his head?"

"If it's a question of the Hunt, yes. His judgment is better than yours."

"You try me high."

"Exactly."

"My god, Head. We nearly killed each other that last time we quarreled. Putting us together—it's ridiculous. Stupid!"

Head's lips twitched. "Have you no tact at all?"

"I can lie as gracefully as anyone. Do you really want that? I didn't think so."

"You might have wheedled a solo from me."

"If I was that stupid, you really would dump me."

"Clever. Having found my weakness, you flatter me by subtle indirection."

"Is there any way I can win in this exchange?"

"No wonder Grey found you a prickly handful."

Aleytys winced. "Very low blow, Head."

"No rules in this game. Did you expect there would be?"

"No." Aleytys grinned suddenly. "I surrender."

"Accepted." Head reached into the desk and pulled out a folder. "Preliminary data on the Hunt in here. Study it. If you decide to accept, meet with Grey in the Library at the sixth hour this afternoon. He'll walk you through the tapes and reports, give you an idea what you can and can't do. I want to see the two of you here tomorrow morning. Tenth hour."

"Right." Aleytys walked slowly to the door. Hand on the massive slab of polished wood, she looked back over her shoulder. "Thanks. I think."

Aleytys yawned, smiled sleepily. "Sunguralingu. Nice name. When will we get there?" She rubbed at her shoulder, still a little sore from the placing of the implant.

Grey let the viewer fold back into the chair arm. "Couple hours. About sundown, local time."

"Funny thing happened." She frowned at the wide viewscreen over the console.

"It *has* been a quiet trip." He started to smile. "What is it?"

"Fool. Seriously, I've been touched twice by someone there."

"Touched how? Where?"

"Sunguralingu, I think. Hard to be sure. Psi-link. Sensory tie."

Grey looked startled. He swung the chair up and examined the instruments. "This far away? And in the interface?"

"See what I mean?"

"Friend or enemy?"

"Friend, I think. He doesn't like me much, seems to find me revoltingly unfeminine."

"Probably a native. The Vodufa's a back-to-the-primitive movement and pretty damn fanatical about it. You did your homework. You know how they treat women. What are you going to do about him?"

"For one thing, find out more about him. My god, what a reach he's got." She closed her eyes. "He's riding through a windstorm now, bothered about a lot of things. He's heading for Kiwanji, so I suppose we'll be meeting him there."

The sun was going down as Manoreh rode into Kiwanji. The wharves were clogged with incoming barges and the refugees who were streaming up the hill to the temporary barracks set up for them. He waved perfunctory greetings to those who called out to him, but didn't stop to answer the questions they yelled at him. *Faiseh must have come in several days ago*, he thought. *With this much set up already.* He relaxed as he left the last of the shelters and rode through emptier streets, past the market square and the small employees' houses. The air cleared for him; the people here accepted him for what he was. Coming back into this quiet was like plunging into cool water on a hot, sticky day. The little houses were empty, their inhabitants lodged now behind Chwereva walls.

The Tembeat was a mud-walled compound sitting like a wart against the walls of the larger complex that housed Chwereva headquarters. One wing of the gate was open. Manoreh slid off the faras and groaned with pleasure as he stretched tired and aching muscles. He scratched briskly beside the fara's mane and projected PLEASURE. The animal rubbed his nose against the Ranger's shoulder.

A gangly apprentice on duty in the gatehouse grinned down at Manoreh from one of the windows in the guardroom. "Hey, couz, long trip this time. You back?"

Manoreh chuckled. "No, Umeme. I'm really still chasing Gamesh across the grass lands. Little man, you've grown half a meter since I saw you last. How goes the training?"

The boy grimaced. "A lot of sweat and not much play. Wish I could go out like you."

"Time will come. Director in?"

"No, couz. He's over there." Umeme nodded at the Chwereva compound. "Something's up." He grinned. "Not that they tell us students anything."

Manoreh slipped the pouch from his shoulder. "Catch." He threw it up to Umeme's waiting hands. "See the Director gets that. I've got something I've got to do." He threaded the faras's nose rein through a tie-ring. "Catch someone passing and have him stable the faras."

"Sure. Anything el. . . . would you look at that!"

A ball of shimmering light arced down across the darkening blue-green-black of the twilight, cutting past the misty ring of moonlets just becoming visible. As he watched the bubble drift down, a thistleweed corolla with a dark seed at the center, he was certain that the dream woman was on board. He ran into the street.

A small groundcar hummed around the corner of Chwereva compound. Manoreh lifted a hand, smiling as he recognized the driver. "Faiseh, couz, hold up."

Faiseh brought the battered little car to a rocking stop, a wide grin lifting his mustache. "Hey, Manoreh, you're back."

"You're the second one to tell me that. I begin to believe it."

"Damn hares marching."

"So I saw."

Faiseh thrust his arm out the open window and the two Rangers clasped wrists. "Good to see you, couz. Long time."

Manoreh nodded. "Long time." He glanced toward the landing field. The glow was gone. The ship was down. "Listen, let me take car."

Faiseh's fuzzy eyebrows arched. "Why not. Later, though. Got to go to the field first. On duty, couz. You saw the ship."

"Take me with you."

"Climb in. But get a move on or the Director'll have my skin. Important visitor. Very important."

Manoreh slapped Faiseh's shoulder in thanks and went around to the far side. As he slid in, he said, "Who?"

"Chwereva has hired Hunters Inc. Finally dug up some official who could count to ten without taking off his shoes, I suppose." He wove the car through the streets then out the gap in the low screen wall. He snorted with disgust as several hares came out of the scrubby juapepo and hopped along the roadside. "Already here. You ever see so many of them?"

"No." Manoreh stared down at his hands. The hares reminded him of the ghost. His hands felt stiffer already. Instead of anger he felt a deep chill.

Faiseh glanced at him. "What's eating you?"

Manoreh looked up. "Haribu got pushy. Had to split off a ghost."

Faiseh drove for several minutes in worried silence then said, "You going back to swallow it?" He scowled at the hares hopping raggedly through the brush. "You better hurry if you want to get out of here."

"Right. Soon's I see the Director."

"Well, Hunters will beat hell out of Haribu for us."

"If they live up to their reputation. Elders won't let them bring in energy weapons."

"Stupid." Faiseh waved a hand at the increasing number of hares threading through the juapepo and beginning to move onto the road. "A few weapons like that and we'd wipe out those bastards."

"I know, but what can we do? Mention energy weapons to the Council and they'll shut down the Tembeat before you get all the words out."

"Well, we could always go join the crazies on the coast."

The hares were spreading across the road. Faiseh cursed as the car began to wobble over the bodies that disrupted the smooth ride. He relaxed as the car steadied over the metacrete of the landing field. The mild current fed into the outer strip was enough to keep the hares off, but they circled it in a solid ring, twenty deep in spots. Faiseh stopped the car a few meters from the dark oval resting on its belly in the center of the field. He shifted uneasily behind the steering rod. "Hope they get a move on. Feel that?"

Haribu was smothering the field. The air hung still and

heavy. Hard to breathe. Manoreh closed his eyes. *She's there,* he thought. *A Hunter?*

"The lock's opening."

Manoreh opened his eyes. A tall man in a gray shipsuit swung down from the lock and stood waiting. The woman came into the circle of light. Slender and tall, taller than he'd expected. The red hair was braided and coiled tightly around her head. She swung down beside the man and the lock closed behind her.

Manoreh watched her, fascinated, locked to her by the link that had formed as she came here, ghosting in the interface that let ships move faster than light. She came past the man and stopped beside his window. Her face was a pale blur in the deepening twilight but he didn't need light to know her features.

"You," she said. "We've met." Her voice was a surprise also, a warm contralto. He found her confusing. She seemed to him both man and woman. Cool and independent and at the same time. . . .

"I know. Why?"

She swung around, facing away from the car. "Later," she said absently. He thrust his head out and twisted around to see what she was looking at.

The hares were on their hind legs staring at her. Force slammed out of them, almost visible in its intensity. She shivered. Manoreh dropped back on the seat, gasping, drowning. His hands closed tightly on the edge of the door. In the corner of his eye he saw movement and turned.

The male Hunter had moved quickly behind the woman and put his hands on her shoulders. She leaned against him. Manoreh heard a ripple of clear pure notes, then stared as a crown of light circled her head and a shimmering golden glow sheathed the two of them, then struck outward at the hares.

Abruptly the pressure from the hares was gone. The crown faded. She slumped back against her partner in obvious distress. He lifted her and carried her the two steps to the car. Hastily Manoreh reached over the seat and shoved the back door open.

The Hunter slid the woman inside and then was in beside her, cat-quick and neat in his movements. "Go!" he snapped.

Chapter IV

★ ★ ★ ★ ★ ★ ★

In the guest quarters at Chwereva Compound the two Rangers stood quietly waiting as the Hunters settled themselves in. Aleytys followed Grey into the bedroom.

He turned to face her. "What happened back there?"

She stepped around him and sat down on the end of the bed. "First touch of the enemy. Chwereva was right, this isn't a matter of animal instinct. There's an intelligent brain directing those attacks."

"Bad? That damn thing doesn't show in public unless you're hurting."

Aleytys lifted her hands and examined them, an excuse for not looking at him. The diadem had been the focus of too many bitter quarrels. "Bad," she said dully. "I'm still shaking."

He leaned over and touched her face. "Find out anything more?"

"Not really. Just that he's horribly dangerous, our enemy. And, of course, that he's got a pipeline into Chwereva. He was waiting for me."

"Not thinking, Lee. Why wouldn't he be waiting, having arranged for you to be here. Can you handle him?"

"Head to head?"

"Yes." He walked to the door, then stood there looking back at her. "Can you?"

"I don't know," she said slowly. "I don't know enough about him, whoever or whatever he is." She eased down on the bed and stared up at the ceiling. "That Ranger out there, the long one. He's my contact. There's a kind of link joining us that both of us are finding very uncomfortable. Could be a complication."

He tapped the wall behind him. "We've got to report in. Let me handle that. You get straightened out with your

35

Ranger. Get what you can out of him, he'll probably know
more about the local situation than the Reps."

"Grey."

"Um?"

"It's . . ." She sat up. "It's been good seeing you again.
Thanks."

"What for?" His left eyebrow arched as he watched her,
skepticism cutting deeper lines in his face.

Aleytys rubbed at the nape of her neck. "For being a thorough professional, I suppose."

With a slight shake of his head he went out.

Aleytys sat on the bed wondering if he'd ever trust her
again, wondering if she wanted him to. Then she brushed the
tiny tendrils of new hair back from her face and stood. Time
to get to work.

She stopped in the doorway. The Ranger was sitting on the
couch. A tall man. Worn, silver-green skin. Scale marked.
Eyes so dark a blue they were almost black. Slit pupils like a
cat's. Firm, wide mouth. A beaked nose. He wore a thong-
laced leather jerkin, torn in two places at the shoulder and
marked with a spot of blood by a half-healed cut on his arm
muscle. His leather shorts were cut off just above the knees.
His boots were scuffed and battered, a tough, hard-used, wary
man. He definitely didn't like her but there was that link that
bound them together, that almost joining of the two nervous
systems. He was uneasy, beads of sweat clinging to his forehead. He swallowed. She could feel the muscles of her own
throat tensing. Nerving herself, she walked across to him and
touched his shoulder.

"Don't!" He slid away along the couch, surged onto his
feet, and stood looking about like a caged chul cat. Abruptly
he swung around and jerked a section of the drapery aside.
With controlled violence he shoved open the glass door behind the wall hanging and plunged into the darkness outside.
Aleytys looked down at her hand with distaste. She rubbed
the hand against her hip. "Professional," she muttered. "Get
the information."

She pushed through the drapes and stepped out into a
small enclosed garden. Automatically she slid the door shut
and searched the shifting shadows among the plants. The
darkness was greater than she'd expected. She glanced up and
was startled by the emptiness overhead. It was one thing to

read statistics about the absence of stars within visual range and another to see the barren sky.

The Ranger was standing on the far side of the garden, close by a spiky tree. He was breathing heavily, his shoulders hunched over. As she stepped onto the grass, she stopped abruptly. The plants caught up the tension between them and flung it back at her. She blinked, yanked up her shields and moved cautiously toward him. He turned and watched her, his dark eyes stone hard. He wanted nothing to do with her. When she was two steps away from him, he turned abruptly and dropped onto a rustic bench that circled the entwined trunks of the tree. The pointed leaves painted staccato shadows across his face and body. She sat crosslegged on the cool grass. "We've got a job to do."

He said nothing, but sat with his head tipped back against the papery peeling bark. She felt him trying to shut her out.

She yawned. "Damn, I'm tired. Look, Ranger. . . . What's your name?"

His first reaction was a stubborn refusal to speak to her, then a flash of humor lightened his mood. "Manoreh."

She touched her breast. "Aleytys. Hunter." She felt his withdrawal and frowned. "What's wrong?"

"You're a woman." He beat his fists lightly on his thighs in his frustration. He could sense her reactions as well as she could his and her snort of amusement with its accompanying scorn defeated him. "Why do you do this?"

"Manoreh, I think we'd better simply accept that we come from different cultures. That's the kind of thing we could have endless arguments about with neither convincing the other." She smiled at him. "Think of me as neuter if it helps." She swept her hand in a small circle. "Do all your plants do that? Catch and reflect emotion?"

He turned from her with relief. He touched the bush beside him gently, separating out the dark nodes, pushing aside the foliage to show them to her as they sat in the branching of the small crooked limbs. "Small woody plants have these. Like the juapepo brush that covers the valley floor." He stood and shoved aside the tree's branches, letting the dim light of the moonring strike through to touch the dark swelling where the twisted circle of trunks met. "Slower growing and more wise," he said softly. Then he smiled. "There's a child's tale that says an old, old tree lives far to the south and is wiser than old men." He let the branches swing closed and settled back on the bench. "Most animals have some degree of FEELING. Hares the most. That's the problem. Haribu has harnessed their gift and is driving them against us."

"Haribu?" She leaned forward. "The Chwereva Reps said nothing about Haribu."

"Haribu Haremaster." His voice was somber, but there was an emptiness in him, a place where anger should have been and was not.

She waited but he said nothing more. "Well? Who is he? If you know his name, you must know something about him."

"Harbiu." He stared at the toes of his boots. "A name. A touch. Haribu . . . the harewalks started three years ago. My family . . . the first to go . . . harewalks . . . they told you about the harewalks?"

"Yes," she whispered. "They told us."

"The hares came at night. They were all asleep. They had no warning. . . ." He sank into a brooding silence.

Aleytys lay back on the grass, listening as he went on in that dull voice after a long silence filled with the buzzing, whispering noises of the garden.

"I was at the Tembeat, the last year of my training. The Director sent me home before my first short trek. Faiseh my friend . . . Faiseh went with me. The gate was knocked down, the stock moaning for water. We tracked them. My people. They walked until they fell and died. We buried them. One by one. We saw the hare pellets around the houses. We saw the tracks where hare feet had chewed the earth to dust, we saw the green bitten off to the ground. But how could we know . . . later more Holdings went . . . Holdings farther south. We learned this much more, that the hares had some connection with the horror. We lost every Holding south of the Chumquivir. We began to FEEL the touches of the directing mind behind these attacks. We named that mind Haribu. Haribu Haremaster. That's all we know."

Aleytys turned her head and examined his face. "What's wrong?" she said quietly.

He hesitated. She sensed a touch of embarrassment then he said, "I split off a ghost."

"I don't understand." When he didn't explain, she sighed and sat up. "Enough of that. What do you think of Chwereva Company?"

"Why?" She felt surprise, curiosity and a touch of contempt stir in him.

"We—Hunters Inc., I mean—we think there's a strong possibility that Chwereva is involved with this Haribu of yours. At least, someone inside Chwereva is conspiring to clear off the watuk population from this world and open it up for new ownership. Haribu was certainly waiting for us at the port. I don't know yet just how the connection runs, but there are things that make it sure." She chuckled. "Which you will not ask about, if you please. We all have our privacies."

He was puzzled, ignoring her attempt at humor. "The Eight Families wouldn't allow Chwereva to attack us. Even a hint of that and the Company would be dissolved. The Families protect their own." His eyes moved restlessly about the shadowy garden. "The Vodufa society contracted with Chwereva for this world. The only immigrants permitted are strict Vodufa. Except Chwereva employees, of course, and they're only grudgingly allowed. Why should anyone else want this world?" Curiosity drove back the chill and he seemed briefly more human. "The Vodufa got it cheap since there were no large concentrations of minerals. It's a light-metal world, no good for high-tech groups, perfect for Vodufa because of their hatred of technology and their plans for a pure society, a return to the old ways of the stalwart and noble originators of the race."

Aleytys laughed at the scorn in his voice. "That explains why the ones responsible for this attack have used such indirect means to clear the world. A couple of stingships could burn you all out of existence in moments."

"Why attack us?" he repeated.

"Just have to ask Haribu that when we find him."

The surge of life grayed out of him. When he spoke, his voice was dull and tired. "Not much time to find him. In a day or two the hares will be hundreds deep around Kiwanji. The psi-screen will hold awhile, but the men inside?" He rubbed trembling hands together. "How long will it take them to wear out?"

Aleytys shivered. She stroked her temples and grimaced when she felt no response. "I've read the Chwereva reports. Plotting the direction of the walks told you nothing. And the explorations you Rangers made have turned up no other form of intelligence." She paused, then grinned. "Except a children's tale of a wise old tree. No truth in that, I suppose."

"We looked and found no tree."

His serious answer surprised a laugh out of her. "You're certainly thorough." She sobered. "Is there anything else? Anything you can tell me that wasn't in the reports, or you haven't had time to report yet? Feelings? Little things apparently insignificant? Wild guesses?"

She could feel him prodding at his memories, could feel a growing impatience and a growing sense of frustration. "Nothing," he said slowly. Then he lifted his head. "Except . . . coming back across the Jinolimas from the mapping swing this time, I saw hares coming down from the mountains."

"So?"

"There were no hares in the mountains before."

"Ah!" She felt a glow of excitement. "Any other Rangers come in recently? Have they too seen hares where no hares should be?"

He was on his feet and for a moment he stood over her, forgetting his dislike of her. "The first walk," he said. "It was there, by the Chumquivir. And it was by the Chumquivir I saw them four days ago. And I never thought of that. I never thought of that." He stretched his arms toward the empty sky, toward the jewel band of the moonring. "Ahhh! Meme Kalamah be blessed, it's a chance. A chance!" He ran to the door, turned there. "I have to go, Hunter. Thanks." He plunged through the drapes. A moment later she heard the outer door of the apartment slam shut.

Chapter V

★ ★ ★ ★ ★ ★ ★

The hares moved slowly over the plain, a great white flood eating anything their teeth could tear out of the red earth. They swarmed over planted fields, stripping the plants from the earth, digging out even the roots. They tore at the juapepo, ignoring the blasts of pain and fear that ordinarily drove off attackers. They flowed along, leaving desert behind, eating, eating, eating, day and night, never stopping, swarming over the empty Holdings, leaving only the poison-thorned emwilea, turning the fragile valley from dry land to desert, on and on, endlessly, mindlessly moving north, flowing toward Kiwanji.

In the Fa shrine, high above the valley floor, the Fa-men gathered and beat their drums and looked down at the creeping hoard with fear and a queasy satisfaction. For them Fa was purifying the land, purging from the Sawasawa the weak-willed and the evil, leaving the strong survivors to throw aside the last remnants of corrupting technology. When the great haremarch was done, they would start the Vodufa again, living by the work of their hands, working with stone and iron and bronze. The Fa-men watched and saw themselves as the inheritors of the people, the blessed of Fa, the pure ones divinely destined to mould the remnant into a great people. And in the meantime, the Kichwash of the Fa-bands maneuvered subtly for higher places in the pecking order.

On the plain the two wings of the hare herd creeping down both sides of the river began to curve around to circle Kiwanji, visible in blue distance a day or two away.

Aleytys sat still for some time after Manoreh had charged off. The breeze was cool and the sharp green smells of the garden pleasant. She was very tired. The trip out had been difficult. Grey had been distantly friendly, a colleague not a lover. As if he'd never been a lover. She found it harder to flush out of her memory the good times and the bad. Especially the bad times. The quarrels and his demands on her, demands she could not really understand or respond to, that she was unwilling even to try to respond to. Sitting in the garden she felt again the suppressed anger and depression. No one to talk to about it. The Three. . . .

She stroked her temple. For the first time they refused to talk to her, those captive spirits of the diadem. Her friends. "I need you. Harskari? Shadith? Swardheld? I need you. Please?" She closed her eyes and sought them in the darkness of her head. Nothing.

Sithing, she unpinned her braids and combed her fingers through the red-gold mass, smiling with pleasure as the breeze lifted fine strands and blew them about her face. It was good to be back in touch with the feel and smell of living things. She pushed down her discomfort and tried to enjoy the moment of quiet. The garden was filled with quiet night noises, the rustling of the plants, the humming of invisible insects. She stroked the cool grass and felt her brief pleasure draining away. The bushes began stirring on their multiple stems, rattling seed pods in disturbing arrhythmic patterns that had little connection with the gusting of the breeze. They picked up her disturbance and tossed it back to her, snatched it again, and built it and built it until she was alone, unloving, unloved. . . .

She jumped up and ran to the long window-door, the garden turning sour behind her. Where the thick drape hung, the glass was a pale mirror. She touched her face and frowned, examining her features in the ghostly reflection. Her mouth was pinched, looked lipless. Her eyes were dull, set in spreading dark stains. She ran her hands nervously over her body. Her breasts sagged as her shoulders curved forward. There was a roll of flesh around her waist. She stood like a lump.

Shaking, chilled, hands and feet numb, mind numb, feeling bloated, ugly, she turned from the window and moved uncertainly about the garden. Her knees shook. She collapsed in a heap in the center of the grass, holding tight to herself, tears slipping silently down her cheeks, clinging to her skin.

She wept on and on, wallowing in her miseries, the cycle repeating over and over until her body chilled into a physical depression as deep as the mental one.

"Aleytys!" Harskari's annoyed voice cut sharply through the diadem's chime. "Stop this nonsense." In the heavy darkness of Aleytys's mind, the narrow austere face of the long dead sorceress formed around snapping amber eyes.

Aleytys shivered. The diadem was once again the agonizing trap it had been for her in the beginning of her involuntary custody of this soul trap created by a jealous man a million years dead. And the three souls trapped inside were hell-born sprites haunting her, spying on her, never leaving her alone. She tried to block out the waves of fear, anger, hate, despair that washed over her in beats, round and round on an ascending spiral that surged toward infinity.

"Aleytys!" Harskari's disembodied voice was filled with disgust. She waited a moment. "Stop this, daughter." Then the imaged face nodded slowly. "So. I must. Obviously you can't help yourself."

Aleytys felt a nudge. Then she was plunged into silence and darkness, shoved aside in her own body. She protested feebly and was ignored. Crouched in darkness, bathing in pain and horror, she felt her body rise and cross to the glass door.

The door clicked shut behind her and her body dropped heavily onto the couch. Harskari withdrew her control. "Take hold, daughter!"

Weakly Aleytys fitted herself back into her body. The experience in the garden had shaken her badly. In all the trials of a turbulent life she'd never come so close to losing herself. She sat gazing down at hands that opened, closed, and opened again. "You waited long enough to say something."

"You were letting yourself drown." Harskari ignored the complaint and frowned impatiently. "That was wholly unnecessary."

"I suppose so." Aleytys spoke aloud even though the other voice existed only in her head. "Well?" She touched her face, then crossed her arm over her breasts and closed her eyes.

Harskari's amber eyes seemed to retreat and the lines of her face grew hazy. Then other eyes opened. Purple eyes in an elfin face surrounded by flyaway red-gold curls. Shadith the poet-singer. And black eyes in a rugged scarred face. Swardheld Weaponmaster.

"I think it's time." Harskari's voice was taut with distaste. The others nodded.

With her eyes closed Aleytys saw them standing as if in a

dim room with guessed-at walls lost in deep shadow. The three were watching her. She had a sense of being on trial. "What is this?"

Shadith and Swardheld glanced at Harskari then retreated into shadow. Harskari's eyes narrowed. "Aleytys," she said, "we've been with you for over five years now."

"What can any of us do about that?"

"If I knew. . . ." A narrow, dark hand lifted and fell, a quick expression of her frustration. "I'm only an approximation of what I was." Another swift pass of her hand wiped this away. "We wish to make sure that the damage we do to you is minimized."

"Damage?" Aleytys frowned and shook her head. "I don't understand. We are friends. Aren't we?" She swallowed. "We've talked a lot the past few years."

"Ween you needed us." The golden-eyed sorceress did not soften her grim expression.

"There were times when I'd have gone crazy without someone to talk to, someone I didn't have to. . . ."

"Didn't have to pretend courtesy and calm with, didn't have to protect yourself from when you couldn't endure the sight and feel of yourself."

"You helped me."

"You turned us off and on like your vid set."

"No, it wasn't like that. . . ."

"We were your crutch. You didn't need to go out and exert yourself or expose your weaknesses and your ugliness to people who might reject or ridicule you. You didn't need to let yourself be vulnerable. We were there. As you said, we were always there." Harskari sighed and relaxed. Her image wavered, then she smiled.

Aleytys felt a warmth flow through her body as she responded to the smile. She started to sit up, thinking the scolding had ended.

Harskari sighed again. "I like you, Aleytys. If we'd met another way, we might really have been friends." The amber eyes moved to meet purple and black. "Perhaps that's true for all of us. Nevertheless, we have seriously damaged you in spite of our good will. Remember what you shouted at Grey that last time you quarreled?"

I don't need you, I don't need anybody. The memory hung between them for a moment, then Aleytys said, "I was angry, I didn't really mean it."

"Even if you didn't mean it, you wanted it to be true. You're terrified of depending on anyone you can't control. And we've pampered that terror." Harskari looked rueful. "We enjoyed too much our talks with you. We enjoyed too much experiencing life again through you. We encouraged you to depend on us."

"There was so much I had no way of knowing, so many situations I simply couldn't cope with."

"Exactly. So much you couldn't cope with." Harskari's amber eyes sparkled with annoyance. "On Jaydugar you took your first steps from the womb of your childhood. You survived many difficulties on your own. Then. . . ." She sighed, her eyes went dull. "Then we came. After a while it was easier for you to lean on us, to let us pick up after you like overindulgent parents. Instead of continuing to mature, you retreated to the safety of your childhood where there was always someone to protect you from the consequences of your errors and stupidities."

Aleytys twisted her head back and forth against the couch cushions. "No," she whispered. "It wasn't you. My mother said. . . ."

"Ah!" Once again the amber eyes were flashing. "We've heard that excuse a thousand times. Forget it. You weren't raised in your mother's culture. And you've disproved what she said a dozen times. Think, Aleytys! Remember your past! Cold and loveless, hah! Only when you had us to spend your affection on! Take responsibility for yourself, Aleytys. You're the sum of what you think and feel. Your mother, nonsense! You never even knew her. Think of Vajd. He raised you. He holds more of you than your mother ever will. Learn who you are, Aleytys. Open your eyes. Don't let others set your limits." Harskari grew calmer. She glanced once again at the others. A sadness flowed between them. One by one they nodded.

"Head's concern kicked us out of our complacency," Harskari went on. "We chewed the situation to shreds but finally came to a painful decision. We must break this dependency of yours, force you to stand on your own feet. Pick up the threads of your life where we broke them, Aleytys. We will not speak to you again. We will not come to your call. In short, daughter, you're on your own. Farewell." The word trailed off as her image melted away.

Aleytys clutched at the couch, drenched with sweat in her

sudden panic. "Shadith," she called urgently. "Don't leave me. Not all alone. I need you."

"Farewell, Lee." The purple eyes closed and she was gone.

"Swardheld, teacher. . . ."

The Weaponmaster looked tired. "Freyka, I've got very fond of you." He grinned like a hungry bear. "Been times . . ." He shook his head. "Never mind. Good faring, little one. You can handle anything you set your mind to." The black eyes closed and he was gone with the others.

Aleytys dug her hands into the cushions and twisted them, sobbing and afraid. The comforting sense of presence that had eased her for so long was gone. She was alone.

"Lee, what. . . ." Grey's voice.

She brushed hastily at her eyes and sat up. "I didn't hear you come in."

"You were too busy talking to them." He turned away, bitter.

She felt a flare of anger burning, ready to burst at him. "Be glad, then. It's the last time." Her low voice was full of pain.

Without a word he was across the room and beside her on the couch. He pulled her against his chest and held her until her shaking stopped. "Want to talk about it?" he murmured, his breath blowing warm across her hair.

She shook her head, her face still buried in the tunic of his shipsuit. "Not yet."

He stroked her hair, then settled her back against the cushions and slid away himself to the far end of the couch where he could watch her. "What did you learn from the Ranger?"

Chapter VI

★ ★ ★ ★ ★ ★ ★

The hares came on endlessly, creeping through the night. Some were laboring now and would soon die, unnoticed cells dropping from the body of the vast beast. The herd across the river plunged in, swimming and drowning indifferently, moving around the city to settle on the north side. The other herd narrowed and lengthened as the great valley narrowed. Beyond Kiwanji a series of escarpments sealed off the plain and beyond them the mountains rose in pale blue waves. The leaders began to curve about Kiwanji to meet the other hares.

They crouched wearily, licking at bleeding paws and ragged fur, then closed their bulging brown eyes and slept for the first time during the long march. Behind them, still coming on, the great herd crept along, stirring up vast clouds of red dust.

Manoreh glulped at the hot cha but it did nothing to warm the stony chill from his body. He set the mug down on the arm of his chair and relaxed. Across the long common room Faiseh stood looking out a window.

Manoreh slid his fingers up and down the hot glaze on the mug. "See any hares on the coast last time you were there?"

Faiseh turned, looking mischievous. "You come roaring in here like a sand rat's got his teeth sunk in a tender spot. Then you don't say a word for a double handful of minutes. Now you come out with this." He shook his head. "No, couz, I haven't seen any hares on the coast. Nothing much for them there anyway. Lot of rock, no water. Only water's on the islands. 'Less the hares swim, the island settlements are safe enough." He chuckled. "Given they don't kill each other off."

"That bad?"

"Like nothing you ever saw, couz." He moved to a chair

and sat down, lifting his feet to rest them on the other end of the same table. "You going to tell me why you asked?"

"I saw one line of hares after another coming out of the mountains."

"Hunh! So you think Haribu could be in the mountains. Where'd you see them?"

"Going down foothills near the Chumquivir."

"So." Faiseh slapped both hands down on his thighs. "Meme Kalamah, first bit of luck since those walks started." Then he scowled. "We got to get out and go after him. If we have to crawl over the testre Dallan."

Manoreh drained his cup. "He has to let me out to swallow the ghost."

"How you doing?"

"Could be better, couz." He massaged his arm. "Feeling is going. Mmh. Pick up mounts at Kobe's Holding?"

"Why not here?"

"Groundcar. We've got to get through the hares fast."

"You should have left hours ago."

"I know. I meant to."

"But got sidetracked." Faiseh looked down at his broad, blunt hands. "Dallan can be a bastard. He don't like admitting the ghost thing can be done."

"When I hit the guardian of our morals for the groundcar, I'm going to be walking stone." Manoreh grinned tiredly. "He'll come through, bet you."

"Hunh. No chance. Last time I tried betting you I walked away with my skin and lucky to keep it. What about the Hunters?"

"No." Manoreh began pacing up and down the narrow room. "Sending a woman!"

Faiseh shrugged. "That one's worth having with us. Eat Haribu and spit out the bones."

"I don't want her along."

"Never thought splitting off a ghost rotted the brain. At best we can't leave before morning. Want to guess how many hares will be out there then? Got a feeling we'll need the Hunters, her for sure, to get us through. You got any better ideas?"

Manoreh flung out his hands. "All right, couz, they come. Satisfied?"

"Happier than I was. I don't fancy trying to sneak up on Haribu with a couple of darters and a lot of hope."

"Fool."

"Start practicing, couz. You got to get it right, got to look like you're about to freeze solid, or Dallan will miss the point. He's not too bright, the dear little man."

Manoreh grinned. He began walking again, his movements getting stiffer and more unnatural. When Faiseh pronounced him convincing enough to be sure Dallan would notice something was wrong, Manoreh grinned at his friend then stalked stiff-legged out of the room.

Chapter VII

★ ★ ★ ★ ★ ★ ★

The predawn morning was cool and quiet. In the flickering light from the single torch, the groundcar was a featureless shadow humming quietly beside the dark guardtower. Aleytys rubbed her hands along her arms, a little chilly but enjoying the crispness of the air. She felt apprehensive and elated at the same time, anticipating the beginning of her first Hunt. She glanced at Faiseh who was shifting uneasily from foot to foot, mustache twitching, watching the silent line of small individual houses where the teachers and apprentices lived.

"What's keeping us here?" Grey sounded impatient. Aleytys smiled to herself. He was as jumpy as she was, wanting to begin, resenting the need to hang around waiting uselessly.

"Manoreh," the Watuk Ranger said crisply. His eyes lifted to the sky, paling very slightly along the line of roofs. "I'll go see what's holding him up." Without waiting for an answer he trotted off toward a house on the far end of the line. Its shape was a dark smudge in the deep shadow beside the taller stable.

Aleytys watched the chunky little man fade into the shadow and felt another chill that had nothing to do with the bite of the air. She walked briskly back and forth beside the groundcar with Grey watching quietly, saying nothing, standing deliberately still. He kept his back to the green glow strengthening gradually above the roofs. Aleytys smiled tentatively at him. "Grey. . . ."

"Get the back door open." Faiseh was coming back, supporting his taller friend. Manoreh was moving with considerable difficulty. The stiffness he'd counterfeited before was becoming real. Faiseh muscled him along toward the groundcar. "Move," he grunted.

As Aleytys set her hand on the latch, a slender figure came

50

through the narrow crack in the gate and moved quickly, gracefully to the group by the car. A watuk woman with shimmering silver highlights gleaming along her cheekbones and a long elegance of bone and a grace of movement that enchanted Aleytys and at the same time made her feel once more a lump of mud. The woman wore a long rectangle of patterned material wound around her body and tied in a roll knot over her breasts. "I'm going with you," she said quietly. Aleytys felt the intense emotion behind the smooth face, but the woman spoke without emphasis and stood gently relaxed as she confronted them. "We both are." A small boy came shyly around her and stood looking up at Manoreh.

Faiseh chewed at his mustache. Manoreh scowled. "No," he said harshly. "You'll be safe here."

"Safe!" She lost a little of her calm. Her dark eyes narrowed. "Your son FEELS, Manoreh. I wanted to tell you that the past months. You weren't there, were you? You want Kobe giving him to the Fa-men? He will when he finds out. You know how he feels about the wildings. How long will it be before everyone knows, locked up together like we are? I can't take a breath that's not shared by a dozen others. Already Gerd and Minimi are watching him. You didn't bother to ask about him yesterday, did you? You had time enough at Kobe's Holding to say a word to me. But I wasn't important enough for you to bother about, was I, when you had a world to save?"

Manoreh brushed his hand across his eyes. "Kitosime," he began.

With a degree of difficulty Aleytys found hard to understand, Kitosime thrust up a hand, the first urgent near-awkward gesture she'd made. It stopped him. "Kitosime," she said. "Your wife. Or have you forgotten that too?"

"The hares." He looked desperately tired. "Too dangerous. I can't stay with you, Kitosime. I can't."

"When did you ever?" She picked up Hodarzu who was clinging, sleepy and silent, to her leg. "I want my son to live," she said quietly. "Kiwanji is a death trap for him now. Do what you have to, Manoreh. But get us out of here first." She rubbed her hand gently up and down her son's back and he murmured sleepily. "You owe us that at least, Manoreh. Get us out of here and leave us at Kobe's Holding."

Manoreh closed his eyes. Through the link Aleytys felt anguish and uncertainty, a fading ghost of the watuk blindrage.

Without stopping to think she left the car and put her hand
on the watuk's arm, the healer in her responding automatically and irresistibly to his need. She closed her eyes and
tapped into the power river, letting the black water pour
strength into him. It wouldn't stay long, seemed to wash off.
When she'd done as much as she could, fighting against a
resistance that negated much of what she tried, she opened
her eyes and saw him looking down at her, startled and re-
pelled. Hastily she stepped away.

She walked back in spite of Grey's disapproval, smiling
ruefully.

Manoreh leaned against Faiseh's shoulder. "Come then," he
told Kitosime. With Faiseh's patient assistance he stumbled
into the groundcar and lay back against the seat. Grey
brushed past Aleytys and sat down next to him. Wearily
amused, Aleytys settled in the remaining corner and took the
small boy on her lap so that Kitosime could slip in and seat
herself on the floor by the Hunter's feet.

When they were all in, Faiseh twisted back over the seat.
"Once we're out of the compound I'm moving fast. Kitosime,
keep your head down. Folks out there aren't going to like a
groundcar going out of Kiwanji. But they won't stop at disapproval if they see you. You got that?"

"Yes."

Faiseh drove slowly through the shadowed streets passing
only a few boy gangs running furtively. "Starting already," he
muttered. There were men sleeping in the narrow lanes between the temporary shelters. Some woke and cursed him but
he ignored them and threaded through the staggered buildings
until he reached the perimeter of the psi screen and the low
stone wall that marked it. There was a gap in that wall where
the road went out of the city. He stopped. The car rocked in
place, humming raggedly. He was sweating, muscles tense.
He shifted in the seat and looked at the silent figures in the
back. "You see them?"

Aleytys leaned forward. The hares were a restless white
blanket bobbing up and down in spots, the far edge beyond
view. The force driving out from them sent bright ripples like
heat waves shivering up and down the force dome.

Faiseh gripped the back of the seat. "Hunter." The tip of
his tongue traced the clean-cut curves of his greenish lips.
"You backed Haribu off at the landing field. Think you could
hold us till we're through them?"

"I can try." She settled in her corner as comfortably as she could, wincing as her feet struck Kitosime's crouched form. "Is there any reason Kitosime needs to stay hidden now?" She pulled her feet back. "I'm kicking her every time I take a breath. That can't be very comfortable."

Faiseh frowned at the emptiness around the car. "All right. Be quick. Climb over the seat, woman." He leaned forward over the control stick. "Hurry."

As Kitosime clambered awkwardly over the seat back, then fished Hodarzu up and settled him in her lap, Aleytys began the breathing exercises Vajd, her Dreamsinger lover, had taught her. She relaxed until her heart was beating slowly, until her breathing was deep and slow. The black water flowed around her; her symbolic image gave her access to the great pool of power winding between the stars. "Go," she breathed.

The car skimmed through the wall-gap and popped through the psi-screen. The harepower struck like a hammer and rebounded from the bubble she held around the car. Force rammed into the bubble, punching like fists at her. Again and again the ram came, driving great dents into her silver bubble, dents she smoothed out with sheets of black water. If the mind behind the ram had been able to shift the point of pressure more fluidly, it might have crushed her. As it was, she had just enough time to counter each of the probes.

She held the bubble until a hand touched her shoulder and Grey's voice came to her from a long way off. "Relax, Lee. You can relax."

She sighed and let the bubble collapse. The black water melted away. Shifting to relax the cramp in her muscles, she murmured, "How long to Kobe's Holding?"

He touched her cheek, smiling down at her. "Should be there around sundown today." He nodded at Faiseh. "According to him."

"Good." She let herself go and all the accumulated fatigue of the past week let her sleep.

Chapter VIII

★ ★ ★ ★ ★ ★ ★

Umeme leaned against the window of the guard tower, frowning as he listened to a growing noise coming from the shelters. The boy wondered if the clamor had anything to do with the groundcar that had left the Tembeat early that morning. He looked out again from the street-side window. More and more men were stopping and staring up at him, scowls on their faces. They clumped in groups of three and four and stood muttering sullenly. Behind them, in the direction of the shelters, Umeme heard a dull roar. It was coming closer. He opened louvered shutters and edged out, looking back along the street. At the sight of the mob of watuk yelling and waving rifles as they ran toward the Tembeat, he hastily pulled back inside and threw his weight on the alarm bell's rope.

The clangor rang out over the yelling. The students and teaching Rangers poured out of the Tembeat and the small houses. They gathered in the court beside the guard tower.

Excited and incoherent, Umeme danced about in the doorway. He managed to spit out, "They're coming, a mob, a bunch of Holders, they're mad about something, yelling and waving rifles." He paused and gasped. "Old Man Kobe's in the middle of them, looks ready to burn the place down."

"Quiet." The Director stood on the steps of the Tembeat main building, frowning at the milling crowd in the court. "Walim Ktaieh, get the boys back in the Tembeat and keep them quiet. Walim Agoteh, get the rest of them armed and get back here. All of you, be quiet. I'll do the talking." He stroked his ash-colored beard, as he waited for his orders to be carried out.

When the court was empty he walked to the guard tower, climbed the ladder and moved to the window, pushing the shutters open as Kobe and his men arrived. Before the Old

Man could bring the butt of his rifle against the timbers of the gate, the Director leaned out, resting his weight on his still brawny forearms. "What do you want, Old Man? You've got no business here."

Kobe glared up at him. "I want my daughter, wild man. Send her out."

Umeme stared open-mouthed at the Director, started to speak and stopped at the quick commanding gesture from the older man. The Director shook his head. "We've got no women here. You know that."

"That whoreson Manoreh has her. Get him out here. Make him send her out." Kobe was turning a purplish blue and his voice was a shriek. He teetered dangerously on the edge of blindrage, ready to plunge them all in blood.

"Manoreh's not here." His old voice was beginning to sing, working on them with all the skill his decades had taught him. "He left this morning, Old Man Kobe, this morning, with Faiseh the Ranger and the Hunters, Old Man Kobe. You may come in, Old Man Kobe, come in and see for yourself." He kicked Umeme in the leg and the boy ran to the pull rope that would trip the counterweight and lift the bar. "Come in and see."

The gate swung open a little, startling a watuk who'd been leaning on it. Umeme held his breath. The thought of those bigoted angry men scrabbling through the Tembeat made him sick to his stomach.

Kobe looked at the Tembeat gates with an expression of deep disgust. He spat and turned away, the double dozen men with him spitting in their turn and wheeling to follow him back to the barracks. Not all the men left. A number lounged against walls, staring and brooding, occasionally speaking to neighbors.

The Director watched the mob shuffle off then leaned back against the window frame. His shrewd eyes examined Umeme's face. He smiled as the boy shifted uneasily. "Well?"

Umeme stared hopelessly at narrow naked feet and said nothing.

"Did Manoreh take his wife with him? Dallan told me about the ghost and the groundcar. He said nothing about stray wives."

"I didn't see her." Umeme met the Director's calm gaze, lowered his eyes. "At least, I didn't see her actually get into the car." He shuffled his feet. "Dallan said I was to open the gate for them; he didn't say count them."

"I'm not Dallan, young friend." Then the Director chuckled. "Keep your mouth shut about this." The hooded indigo eyes twinkled with mischief. "Done a good job of that so far. Now, not even to your best friend, you hear?"

Umeme nodded vigorously. "I hear."

The Director took another look out the window. He sighed as he saw the loungers across the rutted street. "I wonder how it's going to end." Sighing again, he went out and began climbing down the ladder. Umeme stood in the doorway and watched him walking tiredly across the courtyard, moving past the small group of silent teachers with a nod but no words.

Chapter IX

★ ★ ★ ★ ★ ★ ★

The groundcar moved through long shadows and turned into the gate left open when Kisima clan left Kobe's Holding. It jolted through the twisting deserted street of the bound quarter, turned along the wall, then cleared the arch by a hair. Faiseh stopped the car by the well and climbed out, stretching and groaning. Aleytys stumbled out, breathing deeply of the cool dry air, stretching in her turn, laughing a little from the sheer joy of moving about after so many hours sitting cramped. Behind her she heard assorted grunts and sighs as the others unfolded after the long, rough ride. Then Kitosime ran past her, up the stairs and into the house, Hodarzu in her arms.

Aleytys swung around. "What was that about?"

Faiseh snickered. "Bladder. Kitosime likes her comforts."

Aleytys grimaced. "She's not the only one." She followed the watuk woman into the house.

When she came out Grey was prowling about the courtyard, examining the designs on the tiles and peering down into the great Mother Well. Faiseh stood in the archway, shaking his head over the devastation dimly visible in the slowly brightening light of the moonring. Manoreh still sat in the back seat of the car. A stone man half dead. Aleytys crawled inside. Kneeling on the seat beside him, she touched his face, then slapped him hard. He showed no response.

She sat back and regarded him, filled with impatience and frustration. Repeatedly during the ride she'd tried healing him, letting the black water flow into him. It went in and through. An endless drain, passing through and beyond him, not even touching him, as if his flesh were little more than cloudmist. For the first time her healing had failed. She backed out of the car and stood leaning against it, head down. Grey was watching her. He came to her and rested his hand on her shoulder.

"He alive?"

"Barely." She laid her hand on his. His warmth drove some of the chill out of her. "I can't help him."

"You all right?"

She wrinkled her nose. "It undermines. You know?"

"A little. What now?"

Faiseh approached. When he heard the question he touched her arm. "The Umgovi Cluster will be up in another hour." He pointed at the moonring strenghtening into full visibility as the last traces of sunset washed away. "Be a lot of light." He jerked a thumb at the car. "Even in that wreck you could get Manoreh to the ghost in about six hours."

"Me?" She backed up until she was pressed against Grey. Her eyes slid to the dark figure in the car and she shivered. "No." She shifted her gaze from Manoreh and faced the other Ranger. "Why me?"

Faiseh spread out his hands. "Who else can? The reason he split off the ghost in the first place is Haribu was after him strong. Me, I'd go down fast if the demon took me on." He nodded at Grey. "Your companion there, I don't know about him. But you I've seen fight Haribu off. And we all need faras and provisions for the trail. Hunter and me, we can take care of that easy enough. But Manoreh can't wait. You take him."

Aleytys nodded reluctantly. "You've made your point." She stepped away from Grey, feeling a little lost as the pressure of his strong body left her. "How do I find the place? He won't be much help." She indicated Manoreh.

"Come here." Faiseh walked around the car to the driver's side. He reached in and fingered a dial. "Just keep that pointer halfway between south and east once you're out of the gate and clear of the hedge. Take the car up a little to clear what juapepo the hares left, then keep on until you run into something the car won't climb. Then get him into the barn. You know what a barn is?"

Aleytys chuckled. "Yes, Ranter, I know what a barn is." Slowly she turned, looked around the shadowed courtyard. When she faced the car again, she yawned and stretched. "I'd better get started." She grimaced at the rusty, battered groundcar. "I might have to haul him half the way on my back."

Faiseh grinned at her. Grey nodded. "We'll be along some-time before noon," he said. His eyes twinkled at her and he scowled. "Then we'll plot our attack. Haribu beware, the Hunters are on your trail." At Aleytys's sudden laughter, he beat his hands together. "Be serious, wench, or I'll be forced to chastise you."

Still chuckling, Aleytys slid into the car and started the whining motor. In her amusement over Grey's fooling, she'd lost the revulsion and touch of fear that Manoreh's frozen body sent shuddering through her. As she eased the car out through the arch, she was smiling, warm with affection and gratitude.

Overhead, the moonband had widened, throwing a calm blaze of silver-white light over the empty houses of the bound quarter. The uauawimbony tree quivered tentatively then rattled with lusty annoyance as she drove past and turned along the rutted road that angled out toward the Mungivir ferry and the barge landing. After she cleared the hedge, she edged the car around until the needle pointed southeast.

The car began to shudder as it passed over torn clumps of brush and scattered piles of rock. The few leaves the juapepo had left and the limber branches whipped about under the drive of the ground effect, but she ignored that as she ignored the creeping cold radiating from the back of the car. The hours passed slowly, marked only by the progress of the bulge of the moonring across the empty sky. When a stand of trees and the roofs of a cluster of buildings thrust up through the deadly sameness of the flat valley floor, she sighed with relief. Her arms ached from wrestling the car over the uneven surface.

It steadied briefly as she broke onto another red dust track. Before she could react, she was bouncing over the brush on the far side. She muscled the car around and drove along the track, past shaggy emwilea struggling from a once barbered hedge. At the broken watchtower and crumbled gate she turned into the lane toward the solid weather-scarred house through the broken ghosts of the bound quarter huts. As she slowed outside the courtyard arch she heard a stirring in the back seat and felt a slightly stronger flicker of life. She halted the car in a swirl of tattered leaves beside the Mother Well.

In the light from the sinking moon cluster she saw a walled court much like the one at Kobe's Hold. It was crowded with layers of old leaves and dried weeds, the patterned pavement visible only where the decaying mulch had been swept away by the car's passage. There was a musty, abandoned smell circling through the heavy night air. The court was eerily silent now that the whine of the motor was stopped. Aleytys shivered then probed cautiously with her mind, searching for possible danger. She felt a distant ripple around the edge of her reach as if something might be hovering beyond the horizon, waiting and watching. Then she thought she might have imagined it as the feeling dissipated.

She slid out, the leaves crackling under her feet. When she opened the back door, Manoreh lifted his head and looked at her. "Well." Her lips twitched. "Good to see you coming back to life."

His mouth moved. He shifted a hand a short distance, then let it fall.

Aleytys leaned into the car. "Relax," she said. "Let me take care of this." She chuckled. "Poor baby, hauled around by a woman. You didn't like me much before. I hate to think how you'll see me now." She pulled his legs out. He toppled over. She leaned in again and caught hold of his hands, pulling him up until his long body was draped over her shoulder. Grunting with the weight, she straightened with effort and began plodding toward the barn, silently blessing her Vryhh heritage and the fact that her birth world had a somewhat stronger gravity than this. She nudged the sliding door open and trudged inside.

She propped him against the stanchions and held him upright. "Manoreh!" She slapped him hard across the face with one hand while she held him upright with the other. "Manoreh!"

There was a flicker of response. She slapped him again. "Manoreh, help me! What do I do now?"

She felt a slow growth of awareness, a spread of feeling along his numbed limbs. He blinked filmed eyes and moved slightly. A dry tongue searched cracked lips. His head turned as far as it could. "In there." One hand pointed feebly into the interior of the barn.

"Help me," she repeated. She lifted his hands and curled his fingers over the wood. "Hold yourself up."

He swayed clumsily but he managed to stay on his feet.

"Good boy." She wriggled through the stanchion and stood in the manger. "Now, give me your hand."

They moved slowly into the darkness. The link began to

pulse between them again, rousing as Manoreh roused from his dullness. When they reached the haystack, he pushed her roughly away and staggered toward a dim, red figure that crouched before the moldy hay. She saw the ragged image rise. She saw the hooked beak come down on Manoreh's neck and the claws pierce his body. His arms rose to embrace the ghost. She felt an intense surge of grief-fear-rage, then the surge washed out as the smoke figure melted into him.

His shoulders moved, the stiffness went out of his body, his shakedown was energetic and strongly graceful. She felt a deep sense of well-being flooding through him, felt the drowning emotions rushing through him/her, wild as lightning-kindled fire. He felt/she felt intensely aware of her femaleness/his maleness. He came/she came irresistibly toward her/him. She was strong, warm, soft under his hands. He was furiously alive, alive, alive. His hands/her hands were on her/him. His hard body under her hands warm and strong, strong and hard, their two strengths clashing until she yielded/commanded, let him push her down, moaning, pulled him to her. Shipsuit torn off. Wriggling wildly out of it. Pulled him down to her tearing at the fastening of his shorts. Then he was in her, she around him.

Aleytys smoothed the shorts closed then pulled the jerkin over her head. The room was dusty, with a close, dead smell, but the dryness of the air had kept mildew out of the abandoned clothing hanging in the dead boy's closet. Manoreh's younger brother. He'd been a well grown boy that year he took the walk; the jerkin's shoulders were a bit too wide. But her breasts put a strain on the leather. She tugged at the thongs that closed the neck opening and got a little more room to breathe.

She grimaced in the mirror at her bruised face and her swollen mouth. *You look like a whore,* she thought. She undid her braids and ran the boy's comb through the crimped strands, dropping straw fragments onto the floor. This second reminder of her animal rut in the barn sickened her. She'd been raped before, had learned to endure and shake off violence done to her. This was different. Manoreh had violated her mind and soul as well as her body. She jerked the comb through her hair, cursing as it tore loose snarls from the matted strands. *No,* she thought as she finally dropped the comb back on the dresser and went to sit on the bed. *Not vio-*

lated. Worse than that. I raped him as much as he did me. Like two animals. . . . She shuddered and touched her face. Then she reached for her healing water.

Manoreh sat on the porch sensing the woman moving about the house behind him. The link between them was so strong now he could feel the rubbing of her shorts against her thighs as she walked quickly from room to room. He felt inadequate as he wondered gloomily what he should do about her.

She came out of the house and dropped onto the bench beside him. He looked down at his hands, opened and closed them nervously. "I'm sorry," he muttered. "I didn't know that would happen."

Shifting between amusement and anger, she ignored him. After a while amusement won and he winced as he felt this along the link. It diminished him and he resented that. "I know just how sorry you are. Not very comforting to my self-esteem." She began playing with the neck thongs, staring out at the courtyard, as he fought down a surge of anger.

Abruptly she leaned forward, her whole body tensing. Her eyes were fixed uneasily on the sky to the northeast.

"What is it?"

She started at the sound of his voice, swung around to face him, her blue-green eyes wide. "You don't feel it?" Then she shook her head. "No, you don't. I see that." She stood and walked to the railing at the front of the porch.

Eight carved posts supported the roof, each representing one of the Eight Families. She moved along the rail, pulling fingers nervously through her long red-gold hair. "I don't know." She stopped beside one of the posts and began tracing the symbols with her fingertips. "Sometimes I think I'm imagining it." She shivered. He felt her unease and began to be restless himself. "At night sometimes you see things—shapes—at the edge of your vision; you're never sure they're really there; you keep staring at them; sometimes you're not sure . . . not sure. . . ." She pointed toward the mountains, more or less directly northeast. "There's something out there watching us, I think."

"Haribu?"

She shrugged. "I don't know." She stared northward, reaching out, concentrating, trying to touch the presence flowing elusively about just beyond the horizon.

He felt nothing at first, then something like a brushing across his nerves, there and gone before he could catch hold of it. Then nothing again. Leaving her straining on the porch, he went down the steps to the groundcar. He was hungry and began poking about for something to eat. When he found nothing he slammed the door shut and stood looking around the court. There was no cover on the Mother Well. That hurt most; Mother Well was the heart symbol of the Holding and to see her. . . . Hesitantly he crossed to the coping and looked down. Choked. Half filled with debris. He walked away, moving to the arch. He leaned against the stone and looked out over the churned devastation left behind by the hares.

"Faiseh and Grey should be here soon." She was deliberately ignoring his grief. "None of us thought of food last night."

Manoreh glanced up at the sky. The green-gold morning flush behind the mountains was brightening rapidly into full day. Jua Churukuu was a crushed green half-circle sliced across by the peaks. "I don't remember much about yesterday." He kicked at the muck on the tiles and was abruptly on the brink of blindrage.

"No!" The woman came off the porch, moving so fast she was at his side before he could react. Her hand closed on his arm. Her blue-green eyes were intent on his, demanding his attention. Coolness flowed like water from her fingers, quenching his anger. He tried to pull away but her long, narrow hand had a surprising strength. Suddenly the touch of her flesh nauseated him. She was alien and terrrible, and frightening.

She dropped her hand and stepped back.

"Sorry," he mumbled.

"Forget it!" Her mind was screaming at him: ANNOY-ANCE/ANGER. Finally she spoke, her eyes fixed on the ground, "Neither of us can help how we feel. It's our bad luck we don't have the comfort of hypocrisy." Before he could try to answer, she'd swung away from him and was staring back toward the mountains. "He's laughing at us."

He felt it too, a ghastly chuckling, barely perceptible, coming from something that hovered beyond the horizon. He frowned. "Haribu, but different. I don't know. Like Haribu, not quite the same feel. But he does change his touch. I don't know." He faced the woman. "He's waiting. Why doesn't he strike?"

Her eyes had a blank look. For the first time he saw her really frightened.

"What is it?"

"Do you know why I'm here? Why *I'm* here?" He shook his head. "Of course you don't; stupid of me. I'm the bait in this rat trap. That thing out there, he wants me. He arranged to have *me* sent on this Hunt. I'm part of the price for his services to those who're trying to clear off this damn world."

Sick, shaking with her fear and his own, he caught her arm and pulled her toward the car. "Get back to the city. Get off this world. A woman! What the hell were your people thinking of sending you out on a thing like this?"

With that disturbing strength she pried his fingers loose and stepped away. "You don't understand. How could you?" She stepped back from him, amused again and irritated at him. "You've got no idea what I'm capable of. Manoreh, if I give up now, I lose more than. . . ." She sighed. She was right. He didn't understand her; even when he felt every emotion she experienced, he didn't understand her.

"Hunting means freedom to me, Manoreh. What would you do if you were shut, um . . . in this courtyard and compelled to spend the rest of your life in it, vulnerable to every force that wished to twist and destroy you?" She was fierce and wild just then; he backed away from her. "No. I'd face more than your Haribu," she went on more calmly, "to avoid a fate like that." Her hand went up and rubbed at her temple, a habit she had; he'd seen her do it a number of times and each time he felt a cold loneliness in her. Once again she shook off the malaise, then smiled. "This bait is going to give our friend out there a hell of a bad time. If he swallows me, I promise him the worst bellyache he ever had."

He laughed, surprised by her sudden humor. Then rubbed his stomach. "Wish you hadn't mentioned swallowing."

She grinned at him, in control of herself again, beginning to savor the excitement of the Hunt. She turned her head in a sudden flurry of clackings. The uauawimbony tree. Manoreh stiffened, waited, then relaxed. "The others. They're here."

Chapter X

★ ★ ★ ★ ★ ★ ★

Kitosime held her sleepy son tight against her as Faiseh and the Hunter rode through the arch with spare mounts and a pack-faras with supplies for the Hunt. She stood stiffly on the porch long after they had gone, even after the uauawimbony's clatter died away.

Hodarzu whined his discomfort and began wriggling and twisting, knocking his strong, small arms and legs into her tired body. She shifted her hold and lowered him to the floor. "Hush, toto," she murmured. She brushed her hand across her face and grimaced at the film of dirt and sweat on her palm. "Tomorrow, my son, we organize some things. Now we put you to bed. The dirt will wait."

She took the small, damp hand and pushed the door open. The emptiness and darkness was like a wall. For a moment she couldn't gather the strength to break through it. Then Hodarzu tugged at her hand. He was tired and wanted familiar things about him. The two of them moved into the great hall. Their footsteps echoed eerily, sending shivers along Kitosime's body. She swept Hodarzu up, and hurried to the stairs, moving faster and faster as the darkness crept inside her and stirred ancient terrors. For the first time in her life she was alone. Alone in this great house built to hold dozens of families. She ran blindly at the stairs.

Halfway up the first flight she stumbled and fell to her knees. With Hodarzu crying loudly in his own terror, pressing his face into her breast, she got shakily to her feet and stood clinging to the railing until the weakness went out of her knees and she stopped shaking. Hodarzu stopped his wailing as she regained a little calm, reminding her forcefully that he FELT what she felt. She began climbing again. Past the second floor, then the third. To the fourth floor and the snug corner room Kobe's favoritism had given her.

She pushed the door open. Hodarzu's small bed with its high railings was visible in the moons' light coming in streaks through the louvered shutters. The boy was heavy on her hip, breathing noisily in a deep sleep. He muttered briefly as she lowered him into the bed and worked off his crumpled smock but didn't waken. She ran a caressing hand over his springy curls then pulled a light cover over him.

She moved to the window and opened the slats. Later she'd have to hunt out lamps and candles, and see if she could harness a faras somehow to the hand pump to keep the tower cistern filled. She smiled ruefully at the shadowed garden below. So many things to see to. *And I'm so terribly ignorant about all of them*, she thought. After another look outside, she closed the louvers partway, then wandered about the room idly remembering old days, old ways. She slid the closet door back and ran her hands over the dresscloths hanging like ghosts inside. She shivered and shut the door.

Old ways. Old days. Light was falling on the bed in long silvery lines. The old ways. Her eyes moved across the ladder of moonlight on the embroidered bed cover. The hares. May they all be cursed, those men. Not her business. Not woman's business. Go off and leave the women to wait and . . . and . . . her hands clenched into fists.

She looked again at the fine silver lines crossing the bed cover. *Like bars locking me in*, she thought. Without understanding why, her mind went back to the day when Old Man Kobe sent for her, already the favorite among his daughters. She went as slowly as she dared to that big, dark, cool room where her father waited. Rumors had been hissing about the fifth-floor dormitory for months. Kitosime was marriageable and a marriage had been offered. Names were whispered. The other girls teased her without letup, naming absurd candidates, an old man who'd worn out three wives and had two others still in his quarters, another who was a year younger than she and feebleminded besides. She went down the stairs with elegant grace, hiding her fear and her excitement behind the first of her doll masks.

Kitosime closed her eyes. Hodar's wild son, he'd told her. The one who'd gone to the Tembeat. A wilding barely reclaimed. She remembered her sisters and cousins giggling in secret over the rumors, remembered Kobe's barely suppressed hatred and her own fear. And her ultimate sense of worthlessness. She was Kobe's professed favorite; he'd spoiled her, caressed her, adored her. And now he was selling her. She stood before the Old Man that day, eyes meekly on her feet, quivering with outrage; her father was yoking her to one more tainted than herself and she knew why. He wanted the land. Manoreh was Hodar's heir. And for this he would sell his pet. With bitter resentment—more bitter because she was unable to express any of it—she accepted what he told her and moved silently through the ceremonies preceding the marriage ritual.

The first time she'd seen Manoreh—Kitosime smiled and drifted to the bed. She sat down slowly, then lay back, the lines of light curving up over her body. He was standing by Hodar's side in the center of the courtyard, standing beside the Mother Well, waiting for Meme Kalamah's blessing. A fine, strong handsome man.

Her hand moved across her face, then down along her neck. *We were happy*, she thought. *Wildly happy. Tender with each other. It was magic to me then how he knew me. I didn't realize. . . .* Her hand fell away onto the bed cover. She stroked the stiff material then made a fist. *I had to ask*, she thought. *And he had to tell me.* FEELING. *The ultimate violation. And I couldn't handle it. Our first quarrel.* She closed her eyes and lay very still. *The first of many. If only he'd gotten me out of here. He could have. It was so easy for him. He didn't have to stay. Ah, Meme Kalamah, how I missed him that first time. And all the other times. Why didn't he. . . .* She sat up. *I can't stay here. Too many memories.*

In the darkness outside her room she hesitated. She was exhausted but her mind was running in tight circles. She rubbed her hand across her forehead then pulled it around and rubbed at the back of her neck. *Something. . . .* The heights called her, she felt the pull, like strings on her shoulders. She moved quickly to the stairs and climbed to the fifth floor, the dormitory level. She crossed the long hall to the last flight that went up onto the roof.

And stopped—hand reaching toward but not quite touching the warning masks on the newel posts. The pull on her was stronger, almost a compulsion, telling her to step up, to race up to the roof. If she touched foot to that last flight of stairs in defiance of the taboo, there was no going back. She lifted her head, terrified and exhilarated. She felt a destiny calling her, a sense of something tremendous waiting for her. She pushed her hand forward and jabbed her fingers into the mask's carved eyes. She laughed and stepped onto the stairs. The forbidden stairs. She ran up them feeling cloudlight, as if she'd cast off some invisible burden.

The roof was flat. in the center was Kobe's shrine, Kisima's power center, the sky counterpart to Meme Kalamah's earth-heart in the court. The great stone tower rising beside the roof was the cistern. Water was pumped up from the well. It also caught rain through a series of baffles that kept debris out. She wondered briefly how much was left in it. But the shrine drew her more strongly. She drifted to the door and pulled it open, feeling daring and able to handle anything. Inside, five powerstones sat in silversand contained by a low curbing. There was a stone basin kept filled with rainwater and a gourd dipper hanging beside it. These were used to waken the stones. She knew that much, though the actual ceremonies were secret. Other details remained hazy as she looked around and she felt no need to step inside to investigate further. She shut the door and strolled over to the wide walkway around the outside of the five-sided roof. She moved to the waist-high railing and stood looking out across the compound to the southeast, wondering if Manoreh had swallowed his ghost yet. He seemed ghostlike to her now, a part of her past. She moved around to the west. The Mungivir river glinted silver in the light from the moonring. The long limber branches of the uauawimbony stirred slightly. The undemanding clacks that touched her ears were almost swallowed by the whispering of the wind. Nothing else moved. It came to her like words on the wind that the old ways were dead. No matter what happened, the old ways were dead for her. Again she felt the disturbing combination of excitement and fear. And also, unexpectedly, a sense of loss.

Hands clutching the rail, she lowered herself to the smooth planks, then loosed her grip. There were good times . . . the sharing with her sisters . . . the small happinesses . . . escaping the rigidity of her training for the warm, friendly noise of the kitchen, watching hands slicing yams, the deep orange slices falling neatly away from the blade . . . before Kobe made her sit beside him and started killing her spirit. She looked through the railings across the empty plain and wept for the good things that were gone. Wept for the small comforts, the certainties that were sunk now in the past, gone beyond reach.

The tears stopped after a while and she leaned her head against the railing, glowing stiff as the last of the night passed. When the sky began to green in the east, she went downstairs to the kitchen to see what she could scratch together for breakfast.

Chapter XI

★ ★ ★ ★ ★ ★ ★

The hare ring faced inward, silent and implacable, individual hares rising at intervals to their hind feet, then returning to a crouch, giving the white ring an eerie movement as if the herd were a single animal breathing in great gulps.

Just inside the flickering psi-screen, bands of boys ran about, hooking hares through the barrier and knocking them on the head. Others darted off with the bodies, taking them to the shelters for the women to cook.

In the streets groups of men lounged about, the groupings swelling and diminishing as restless individuals came and went. The air was thick with a smoldering anger. One man bumped into another and cursed him. They fought, flailing at each other until one staggered off leaving the other tumbled in the street. In another street a dead man was stretched out, steam rising from the blood pooling on the beaten earth.

The tension in the barracks was like steam, thick and hot. The noise was deafening and unending. Bands of boys ran continually through huddled groups of women and old people, sometimes scuffling in play, sometimes exploding into blindrage and battering each other and everyone around. Occasionally they were called to order by some adult still possessing authority. Like the groups of men outside, the gangs split and reformed, the mob growing greater than the individual members, taking on a personality different from many of its components. Wilder and wilder, their humanity slipping rapidly away, the boys gradually took control of the shelters, terrorizing each other and everyone else inside.

Umeme leaned on the windowsill of the Tembeat's guard tower, fascinated and horrified by the disintegration proceeding below him. He was beginning to worry. Men kept passing the Tembeat and the Chwereva complex, muttering ominously, sometimes shaking their fists and yelling obscenities.

The groups were getting larger as the hours passed. And closer to the edge of a blindrage explosion. He lifted his head and stared out at the hare ring. He could almost smell the psi-screen burning under the pressure. The flickering was increasing in frequency as the hours passed. He shivered and pulled back, wishing his time were up. *Three hours is getting to be too long,* he thought. He looked up at the sun and sighed. Half his watch left. He began to pace back and forth from window to window. As he walked, he practiced his lessons, struggled to distance the abrasive emotions intruding from below.

Faiseh grinned down at Manoreh. "In one piece again, huh?" The two men clasped wrists, then Faiseh dismounted. "Any problems?"

"Got a hole where my belly should be. The two of you forgot food when you packed Aleytys off with the car and me."

"'Easy to fix. Come around here."

Aleytys moved slowly away from them. Back on the porch she probed at the presence once more. It was aware of the new arrivals; she could feel the curiosity, the sharpened focus of its interest. She felt more than ever like bait on a fishhook.

In the courtyard Faiseh dug in his saddlebag. He pulled out a round, flat loaf with edges of meat and cheese spilling out and handed it to Manoreh, then fished out another for himself. Talking in low voices the two men climbed the steps and went to sit on the bench to eat.

Grey finally slid from his saddle. He'd been watching her since his arrival, taking in her change of clothes and the fall of her hair. Aleytys rubbed at her nose, acutely conscious now of his eyes and very glad she'd healed the betraying scrapes, scratches and bruises from last night's rutting in the barn. *He knows something happened,* she thought. *His eyes are too sharp and he knows me too well.*

He came up the stairs quickly, quietly, a hunting cat on the prowl. His boots made no sound on the gritty planks of the porch. He stopped beside her. "Ready?"

"What?" The question startled her. She'd been so intent on her own reactions she'd briefly forgotten the Hunt.

He lifted a hand impatiently, then dropped it back. He was full of sharp edges this morning. Poised to move even when he stood motionless. "Lee?"

"Sorry. Thinking about something else." She brushed the

hair back from her face and he grimaced, knowing she used
the gesture to buy time. Aleytys chuckled. "Slow down, Grey.
We've got a nibble. Our fish has been poking around us since
sunup." She rubbed her back against the pillar. "Out there,
vaguely northeast. Give him half a chance and he'll strike."
She frowned at the two Rangers on the bench. "Do we need
them?"

Grey prowled past her, unable to stand still any longer.
"Part of the bait. Camouflage. Know you don't like that.
True though. Time to get back to the ship. Our friend takes
you. I come behind and land him. Right?"

Aleytys stroked along the line of her collarbone, stopping
to rub at the warm spot where the tiny implant nestled.
"That's why Head had this thing rushed." She tapped the
warm spot. "What about your end? Still working?"

"Checked it on the way here. Distance and direction both
sharp." His eyes were bright with mischief. "Don't trust us
yet, do you."

"Being bait makes me nervous." She looked away from
him toward the presence. *Waiting for us. For me*, she
thought. She started shivering, her amusement fading. "Grey,
don't get lost. This thing scares hell out of me. Given half a
push I'd start running and not stop till I had a dozen star systems between me and that . . . that spider out there." She
touched her hair again, then shrugged. "All right. I had to
say it." She left him and walked briskly to Manoreh, her bare
heels thumping defiantly on the planks.

"You feel that?" She jabbed her finger toward the waiting
presence. His answering nod was unnecessary. His uneasiness
matched hers. "We're targets," she said. "Bait, I told you.
Stay with me and he'll take us both."

"What choice do I have in honor?" He brushed at the
crumbs on his shorts. "Let you go alone? No!"

"Don't be a fool. Grey will be following. Stay with him. I
can take care of myself."

Manoreh tapped his head. "I feel him. So he's pinned me,
too. Want me to betray your partner?"

"Damn!" She turned to Faiseh. "What about you?"

Faiseh's bushy eyebrows arched. "Never was as strong a
FEELER as Manoreh. Good thing now. Haribu don't even see
me. Hunter Grey going back to the ship?"

"Grey?"

He was close behind her. "I see where you're heading." He smiled at Faiseh. "Coming with me?"

"Right." He stood and stretched. "We better get started."

Hands on her shoulders, Grey turned Aleytys to face him. "Give us till sundown before you start riding. I want to be close to the ship. And. . . . take care?" Without waiting for an answer he followed Faiseh down the steps and slid into the front seat of the groundcar beside him. Minutes later the whine of the motor was drowning in the clacking of the wimbony pods, then even that sound died away. Aleytys stood still until the spot of warmth under her collarbone faded. Grey was out of her range now and she was left alone with Manoreh. She grimaced in Haribu's direction. "Father of confusion," she muttered.

"What?"

"Never mind." She went to sit down beside him. "Do you have any idea why this tie exists between us?"

"None. Chance, I suppose. Like resonating crystals. Haribu's our striker. When he's gone maybe the link will dissolve." He frowned. "I never heard of anything like this before. Usually communication cuts off after a little distance is covered. Out of sight, out of touch." He leaned back and brooded.

Haribu seemed puzzled, expecting them to move on, and when they continued to sit, talking occasionally, he jabbed at them again and again, as the sun left the mountains behind and slid up into the greenish sky.

After a long silence, Aleytys said, "Your wife is lovely."

Manoreh resented her words; she knew that immediately. He didn't like her talking about Kitosime. "Yes," he said curtly.

Aleytys smiled, wiggled her toes, then yawned. "Point taken. Off limits."

Reluctantly at first, then with words flooding out, he capitulated to her interest and his own worry. "Kitosime. I don't understand her. She's changed. She was always difficult. Wanted me to settle down, leave the Tembeat, take up my father's Holding." He rested his head against the wall and closed his eyes. "This land. She wanted to get away from Kobe. I didn't realize. I never could talk to her. Never tried much. We quarreled. She was drugging herself. Fezza seed, I think. Hodarzu FEELS. We'll have to start training him soon, take him to the Tembeat, don't know how she'll take that, she hates the Tembeat. What's she going to do alone at the Holding? She's never done anything for herself except endless embroidery. How is she going to manage?"

Aleytys put her hand on his arm and snatched it back as the link intensified almost beyond bearing. "Don't be stupid, Manoreh. The Kitosime I saw in that car will do what she has to do to survive. If she has a little time and isn't forced to react on instinct, she'll figure out what she doesn't know. Believe me, it's not that hard. I was raised in a house a lot like this one. Like Kitosime I was forced out of a familiar pattern of life into something totally unknown to me." She shivered. "Leave or be burned at the stake as a demon. The choice wasn't hard to make. I went into a wilderness alone with no training whatsoever. And I survived. Kitosime has her familiar house around her. But she won't fit back into the old life once this is over. You'll have to face that, Manoreh."

He was startled and stared at her, his dismay flooding her. He felt her hurting and was immediately sorry, then annoyed as he felt her impatience.

"Don't worry, she won't be like me." Aleytys chuckled. "You make very clear how much that thought charms you. However, I warn you, my friend, if you thought she was difficult before, just wait until she gets a taste of independence." She shook her head. "It's habit-forming."

Haribu began probing again, attracted by the sudden burst of strong emotion.

They sat in silence, side by side, shutting themselves away from Haribu and partially from each other. The sun crept higher and the air warmed.

"Do you have children?" Manoreh asked suddenly.

The pain was immediate and intense. She hadn't thought of Sharl for a long time; it did no good, only made her sick and aching with the loss of her baby. Manoreh's uncomprehending remorse broke into her pain. She sucked in a deep breath. "No problem," she said. "I have a son. I haven't seen him for almost four years now. May never see him again. It's a long, complicated story. He's living with his father. He thinks I'm dead. He was asleep beside his half brother last time I saw him. My baby. I. . . ." She pushed at her hair. "I couldn't keep him. He almost died because of me. And there are still . . . my life is too complicated . . . unsteady. He's better off with his father. My cousin is his stepmother, a loving, gentle woman. Brothers and sisters to laugh and play with. A quiet healthy life." She looked down then jumped to her feet and ran lightly down the stairs. By the Mother Well she turned and faced him, "Forget that. It's over and there's no changing what is and must be. And I'm hungry. Any more of those sandwiches?"

Manoreh came slowly down the steps, frowning, confused. "I thought you and the other Hunter were wed."

Aleytys ran her fingers through her hair and laughed. "No indeed. He's my boss." She danced to the patient faras and began working at the straps holding saddlebags shut. "I'm a poor, downtrodden apprentice, Manoreh, trying to earn my independence. Umph." She touched the rough texture of a round loaf. "Don't you believe in wrapping these things?"

"He doesn't act like that." He took the sandwich and held it while she brought out the last of the loaves.

"You're misreading. Watch that, friend." She sank her teeth into the bread and tore off a mouthful. Then walked slowly back to the porch enjoying the taste of the food.

"I don't understand."

Aleytys swallowed. "You're an empath and a strong one. But you let your rearing skew your reading." She grinned at him. "I'm not complaining, mind you. If you knew how many times I've fallen over my own feet for the same reason."

A sudden flare of anger from him that held a touch of the madness of blindrage informed her she'd made a mistake with her sympathy. He wasn't prepared to accept fellowship with a woman. "Sorry," she said, "but you see what I mean."

He stalked away, leaving her standing alone at the foot of the stairs. She saw him charge through the arch and vanish around the wall. "Well." She climbed the stairs and sat down on the bench. "You'd better start adjusting a little, my friend, or Kitosime will shock you out of your feeble mind when you get back to her." She took another bite from the sandwich and leaned back, chewing thoughtfully.

Chapter XII

★ ★ ★ ★ ★ ★ ★

The wildings came shyly into the courtyard. Two boys and a girl. Dirty faces, starved bodies, wearing a few rags. Kitosime stood on the porch and watched them sidle around in the morning shadows like small brown ghosts. Fragments of emotion blew across the court. Curiosity. Hunger. Fear. Uncertainty. Desire. And most of all a wistful hunger for affection and mothering.

Kitosime sat down on the top step and wondered what she should do. They were wildings. She didn't want Hodarzu around wildings. But they were children. And hungry. They drew together and huddled against the Mother Well, seeking support in physical contact. She leaned forward. "Don't be afraid," she said, trying to keep her voice soft and welcoming. She smiled at them. Children. Her eyes lingered on the girl with a fascination she was reluctant to admit to herself. Girls weren't supposed to FEEL or go wild. But here was proof, if she'd needed it. She'd suppressed her own ability to FEEL, instinctively sensing its danger. She smiled again. "You must know I won't hurt you."

Wide eyes watched her intently. The boys were bolder. After a few minutes they were grinning at her and edging toward her. The girl remained crouched by the well, watching her, suspicious, yet desperately wanting to trust, needing the warmth and affection she feared.

More urgent than all the complex and contradictory emotions there was the children's demanding hunger.

"Wait." Kitosime walked slowly back across the porch, then fled through the house to the kitchen. The quick-bread she'd attempted earlier sat on the table. A little uneven in spots, but edible. Cheese and meat on a plate waiting for her own first meal. She hadn't tried anything more complicated yet. Hodarzu was still sleeping. She worried briefly about what to feed him. *Better start working on that soon,* she thought. Then she shrugged. *Later.* She cut open three loaves, fought with meat and cheese, hacking off ragged chunks. She put the crude sandwiches in a small basket, added a crock of milk and three mugs.

Wondering if the wildings had understood her enough to wait, she walked carefully through the house, carrying the basket and the crock. She paused just inside the door to order her emotions and quiet her breathing. Then she pushed it open and walked back to the steps.

They were still there, across the courtyard, watching her. She settled herself on the bottom step, holding the basket on her knees and looking at the children. At her smile they edged closer, eyes fixed on the basket. She rested her hand on the basket's edge. "Yes, I have food for you. I suppose you don't remember your names."

The two boys came a bit closer. She could feel them wanting the food but still afraid of her. The girl sidled nearer but stayed several steps behind the boys. Kitosime could feel her terror and her cramping hunger. All the pain of her own childhood was there in the dirty, meager flesh of this small girl. Kitosime looked from one silver-green face to the next, feeling a growing excitement as an idea struck her. "I'll give you names."

They eyed her warily, understanding none of the words and confused by her emotion.

The tallest boy was closest. She pointed at him. He shied but stayed where he was because there was no threat accompanying the gesture. "You will be Amea," she said firmly. "Amea."

He stared at her, no comprehension in his indigo eyes.

Kitosime sighed and turned to the smaller boy. "I'll call you Wame." He was darker green than the other two, with only a hint of silver where the bone was close to the surface of the skin. There was a lively intelligence in his round face, but the name meant nothing at all to him. "Wame," she repeated. She waited. Again no response.

When she spoke to the girl her voice was softer, more coaxing. "You will be S'kiliza. S'kiliza. S'kiliza. Ah, child, understand me. S'kiliza."

The girl shifted uneasily, then she came slowly up and curved her skinny body against the largest boy's side.

Kitosime touched the crock of milk beside her, eyes

thoughtful. "You spoke once," she murmured. "Not so long ago." As she placed mugs by the crock, the boys edged yet closer; the girl came reluctantly with them, still clinging to the largest boy. Kitosime lifted one of the round loaves. "Amea, this is for you."

Both boys rushed toward her, grabbing for the bread.

She dropped it back with the others and hugged the basket tight to her breasts. "No!" She shook her head. Once again she looked from one to the other, demanding their attention. "No," she said more softly. "Before you eat, you'll have to answer to your names." Pointing to each in turn, she named them. Again and again she named them. Amea. Wame. S'kiliza. Their painful confusion and their clamoring hunger touched her like pats of fire, but she kept control of herself and repeated the lesson with iron patience. The sun crept upward and warmed the air in the courtyard as the children squatted on the painted tiles and struggled to understand what was being demanded of them.

Kitosime's shoulders ached and her voice grew hoarse. Her hand moved around the circle again. Again she repeated the names. A spark lighted suddenly in the smaller boy's eyes. He jumped to his feet and waited impatiently for her finger to come back to him and her voice to make the sound. "Wame," she whispered.

He beat excitedly on his chest and nodded. He took a step toward her, still nodding. The other two tried to come with him, but he pushed them back and came eagerly up to her.

Shaking with triumph and tiredness she poured milk into one of the mugs and handed it to him, then gave him a sandwich, suppressing a shudder of distaste at the sight of his cracked fingernails, black with old dirt, and at a wicked half-healed scratch spiraling up his bone-thin arm.

He squatted beside her gulping the milk and nearly choking on the meat and bread. Kitosime closed her eyes a moment, then began the tedious naming once again.

The girl responded next, snatched the food and darted across the court to sit in the shadows on the far side, close to the arch where she felt more secure.

The oldest boy was the last, perhaps because he was older than the others and had spent the most time in the wild forgetting speech. Kitosime watched him, speaking the name she'd given him over and over, hoping for the slightest spark of understanding. Wondering, as she voiced the word, why wildings didn't speak. As far as she knew no one had ever asked himself that question or attempted to find the answer. It was a part of the shame of going wild, a part of returning to the animal. They could speak once. Why did they stop?

Finally the boy stepped forward. She couldn't be sure whether he really grasped the idea that Amea was his name, a sound belonging to him alone, or only responded when she called him because there was no one else left. He took the bread and milk and squatted beside Wame.

Both boys crammed their mouths full, gulped at the milk, the excess dribbling from the corners of their working mouths. Across the court the girl ate just as avidly at first, then glancing repeatedly at Kitosime out of shy-sly dark eyes, she disciplined her hunger and ate in quick small bites, quiet and neat.

Kitosime rose cautiously and moved slowly back into the house for a basin of warm water, some towels and a bar of soap. She settled herself back on the bottom step and waited until the wildings finished their food. Then she called them. Once again Wame was the first to respond. She took his hand gently. Then she began sponging away the grime and stains from his soft young skin.

He projected PLEASURE. and bent down so she could wash his face.

S'kiliza came eagerly to be washed, not waiting to be called. She thrust out grubby hands and projected DESIRE. And sighed with pleasure. And projected PLEASURE, once her hands, arms and face were clean. Amea wouldn't let Kitosime touch him, but he did take the rags and soap and wash himself.

Kitosime stood and walked slowly up onto the porch. *No turning back*, she thought. She pushed open the door and turned to face the children. Fumbling at old barriers she struggled to project INVITATION/REASSURANCE to them. They watched her silently. "Trust me," she said huskily. "Look, I'll wedge the door open." She knelt, found the triangular bit of wood kept next to the wall and shoved it under the door. Then she stood and tugged at the edge of the door, showing them how solidly it was braced open. "You'll be free to come and go." She noted briefly how much speaking aloud sharpened the REASSURANCE she was still trying to project. "Come in," she repeated. "There's no one here but my son and I and he's asleep. You don't have to be afraid." As she spoke she moved away from the great hall.

When she reached the foot of the stairs, Wame slid inside. Amea followed. After another minute S'kiliza came cringing in, terrified to the point of paralysis but driven by a desire almost as powerful. Kitosime went lightly up the stairs bubbling with joy and triumph. At the third landing she looked behind. Three shadows were creeping up the steps behind her. Laughing with delight, she ran up the last two flights to the dormitories tucked under the roof.

The children's place. After she left her baby crib she'd slept here until her marriage. Leaving the door open, she went to the long row of chests lined up under the windows. As she rummaged through the children's clothing left behind when the Kisima went, the wildings came shyly in. She pulled out smocks and shorts for them, even for S'kiliza. A dress-cloth would not be practical for the wild.

With a gasp of joy, S'kiliza ran into the room. She tore off her rags and pulled the smock over her head. With the shorts crumpled in her hand, she streaked out of the room. Kitosime could hear the soft thuds of her feet on the stairs. The boys snatched up the rest of the clothing and ran after her.

Kitosime went slowly down the stairs. She was tired, her legs were shaking, there was a swimming in her head. But she felt a thing unfolding and unfolding within her until she filled the house, went beyond the house, filled the whole present, went beyond the present time into the mythic time with no past, present or future.

She stepped into the sunlight. After the still darkness of the house, the green cool breeze and the brilliance of the sun shattered the wholeness of her skin. Then she was only herself, standing on the porch looking into the silent empty courtyard. The children had vanished. Into the juapepo again. What there was left of it. She closed her eyes and tried to project, remembering and envying the quick fluidity of the children's communication. She felt locked in her head, as if she were suddenly dumb. She tried again, fighting repression, projected WELCOME. And felt the feeble effort drop like a stone into the dust. She remembered her sense that the projections sharpened with speech so she tried again, calling the words into the empty space, letting her hope try to lift the feeling farther. "Come back, please. The door is open. You are welcome, children, my children. You are loved." For a moment she felt, or thought she felt, a fleeting response.

She went back inside to get Hodarzu out of bed and start getting herself settled in the house.

The groups of men standing around in front of the Tembeat compound were bigger on the third day. And they were silent. They walked up and down on the hard-packed earth outside the gates. No muttering. No shouts. No obscenities. And no threats. But the air stank of hatred and rage. That morning the Director stopped the apprentice whose watch it was and sent him back to the public rooms inside the main building. He climbed the ladder, limping a little because an old wound in his leg had begun to bother him again. He sent away the boy on duty and stood behind the closed shutters looking down through the louver slits at the men below. He stayed there around half an hour, then climbed down, sweating and shaking, his nerves plucked raw. Ignoring the greetings of the walimsh and the apprentices, he went into his rooms and locked the door. He lay down on the bed and stared at the ceiling and tried to find a way to escape what he knew was coming. *How long?* he thought. *The boys. What am I going to do about the boys? Got to get them out of here.* His leg ached. He sat up and massaged the scar, remembering the chul cat that made it a long, long time ago.

Out on the street two men threw their shoulders against the gate, recoiled with grunts, shoved again. More men joined them until the massive gate was shuddering against the bar.

Umeme forced himself out of his room. He pushed against the flood of mob-rage, silent and stifling. The air felt thick. When he breathed he felt like panting; there was no life in the air he breathed. He pulled himself up the ladder and looked down at the men throwing themselves against the gate and the others silent and expectant, ready to roll in once the gate was down. He turned and fled, down the ladder and across the court. Into the main building. To the Director's room. He banged on the door and called out. Banged again.

The Director snatched the door open and glared at him.

"They're breaking the gate down," Umeme said breathlessly. "It won't last another quarter hour."

The old man closed his eyes. He seemed to shrink. Then he straightened his body and opened his eyes. "Get the students together in the Long Room. Apprentices and novices both."

His voice was crisp, precise. "Ten minutes. Have them there. You seen walim Agoteh?" When Umeme shook his head, the Director frowned. "Find him. Send him to me. Here. Then wait for me in the Long Room. Got that? Then get!"

Umeme darted off, relieved to have something definite to do.

Ten minutes later the Director limped into the room. The students fell silent and sat staring at him. Fifteen pairs of eyes in puzzled apprehensive faces. "You're getting out of here." Mouths opened to protest. "Shut up. No time to argue. Walim Agoteh is waiting for you in the stable loft. He'll take you onto the roof and slip you into the Chwereva complex." His lined, hairy face was grim. "Chwereva will kick you out if they see you. Don't let them. Understand?"

Umeme burst out, "What about you, Mzee? And the Walimsh?"

"Not your business." The Director tugged at his beard. "We'll do what we have to. Umeme, you're in charge. See that these cubs keep heads down. Got it? Good. When this mess is over, get them someplace safe. You hear? Long as you—all of you—live, the Tembeat lives. All right. Get!"

The Director watched the boys file out. Umeme was last. The boy hesitated, saluted and hurried away. The old man sighed. The end of what he'd tried to build here. He went briskly out to organize what defense he could against the madness that was coming.

Grey felt the tickle in his brain an hour before sunset. He glanced at Faiseh. The Ranger nodded. "Coming up," he said. "We got to go around and hope Haribu don't notice us."

He turned off the road and began circling to the east, moving away from the river. The groundcar whined and bucked and several times labored so slowly along that Faiseh began muttering and glancing about, his face worried. A small herd of hares moved past, sharp square teeth tearing at the sparse vegetation. They looked lean and bedraggled; their ears drooped limply; they ignored the car in their intent search for food. Faiseh's mouth closed tightly. The ends of his mustache pushed down. He stared straight ahead and nursed the car along.

Grey watched the Jinolima mountains come closer as the car got closer to Kiwanji. The city was set at the upper end of the long oval valley, with the mountains rising behind it in waves of blue to meet the paler green of the sky. More small groups of hares rocked past them. Grey examined them with interest. "They look half-starved."

Faiseh grunted. "Don't think about them. Better not to talk at all. Haribu."

To the west Grey could see a shimmering haze, vaguely dome-shaped and barely visible. Kiwanji. The psi-screen. Already faltering. Grey scowled. *This was a damn disorganized hunt. Not going to try this again. Hunt alone or not at all.*

Faiseh began to turn west again. Grey thought about Aleytys and wondered what she was doing. Should be starting out by now. He leaned back. *Yes, she's moving. Northeast. Good.* The dark shoulders of the ship were coming up now over the scrubby juapepo. He relaxed and nearly fell asleep as Faiseh pushed the laboring car along.

There were no hares left around the field. Faiseh sighed with relief and let the car's motor die. It shuddered, gasped and banged down hard on the metacrete. The two men crawled out. Grey stretched and groaned then started toward the ship. "Come on," he told Faiseh. "I want to be inside when your friend Haribu takes the bait."

Faiseh looked nervously at the ship. "Never been in one of those."

Grey smiled. "Nothing hard about it. Remember the first time you climbed on a faras?"

Faiseh chuckled. "If that's supposed to. . . ." His mouth dropped open.

A tall thin man stepped around the curve of the ship. Grotesquely thin. Shimmering like a column of brushed steel in pewter-colored tunic and pipe-stem trousers. He had brilliant red hair and paper-white skin. His greenstone eyes moved from the Ranger to the Hunter "You took your time."

Grey clasped his hands behind his back. "Faiseh, seen anything like him before?" Casually he moved a few steps away from the Ranger.

Faiseh snorted. "He sure's not watuk." He strolled toward the stranger, grinning amiably.

"Think I heard him described awhile back." Grey unsnapped the holster flap and took out his darter. "He was painted up like a watuk then."

The thin man smiled tensely. "That won't work." His voice was like a velvet caress.

"Easy to say." Grey touched the trigger sensor and knew immediately the darter was dead in his hand. Faiseh's simpler weapon phutted, but the thin man fanned an arm through the air, knocking the darts aside with contemptuous ease. Grey dropped the gun and sprang at the stranger, the hand with the stunner implants darting for the side of the stringy neck.

He saw too late the exoskeleton plating the fingers of the withered hands and cupping around the back of the head. His hand slammed against the metal and slid over it; the jolt from the biologic stunner flowed uselessly off along the surface of the skeleton. He twisted desperately as the long narrow hand flicked toward him, its speed blurring its outlines. Pain jarred through him. He stumbled, fell to his knees beside the body of the Ranger, saw the foot coming at him and rolled desperately away.

The man was on him then, feet slamming into him. He caught glimpses of the smiling face as he scrambled away from a punishment that was turning his body into mush. A sense of futility began to drain away his resolution. He just had time for a fleeting regret about Aleytys walking into a trap without the backup she needed before there was a final explosion of pain.

Chapter XIII

★ ★ ★ ★ ★ ★ ★

Kitosime eased out of the barn trying to keep the yoked buckets steady. I was harder than it looked since they had a tendency to start swinging in off-balance circles. She put a hand on the ropes and took a cautious step down the path to the house, hardly daring to breathe. She remembered the boundwoman Drinnis trotting along this path a dozen times each milking, laughing and calling jokes to the other milk-women. Sometimes Kitosime wondered if she'd ever move with that spontaneous joy in the body after the years of smothering. Or FEEL with the rapid rippling fluidity of the wildings after the years of denial.

Milk splashed on her foot. She stopped, steadied the buckets, trying to hold the yoke rigidly horizontal. She'd have bruises on her shoulders and hands tomorrow. She glanced up at the sun. The western sky was greening, only the top of Jua Churukuu still visible above the emwilea hedge. The day was almost gone. As the buckets quieted, she stood smiling at the twilight shadows in the kitchen garden, saved from the hares by the high stone walls around it, stood breathing in the pungency of the herbs growing beside her feet. Stood delighting in the silence and solitude.

She'd worried about that on the way out here, worried about being alone. Foolish, she thought. She laughed and the sound rang pleasantly in her ears. She settled the yoke on her shoulders and walked through the lengthening shadows toward the kitchen door. Her muscles were relaxed now; she fell into a steady rhythm without thinking of it and moved lightly along the tiled walk.

In the kitchen she set the buckets down beside the door leading down to the cold cellar. Then stood looking around the room. What to do for supper? She was getting very tired of meat and cheese meals and Hodarzu should have hot food.

85

She poked at the beans simmering in a pot at the back of the wood stove. Sitting there since morning and still hard as rocks. How long did it take to cook the cursed things? Maybe some soup. Meat from the cold cellar and vegetables from the garden. The thought made her mouth water. She rummaged through the pots and pans, found one that looked suitable, filled it with water. She mangled off some chunks of dried meat, enough to cover the bottom, then went out to see what she could find in the garden.

She had to light the kitchen lamps before she finished washing and chopping up the vegetables for the soup. She dumped everything into the pot, added a pinch of salt and some herbs, then set the pot on the simmer shelf beside the beans. She stood back and frowned at it. "I hope you cook a little faster," she said, giving the bean pot a dubious look.

Hodarzu, she thought. *Time to bring him in.* She'd left him playing in the water garden. Patting a yawn, she slumped through the house. She was pleasantly and thoroughly tired; she'd worked her body harder today than ever before. But her mind was calm. All day she'd felt her nerves relaxing, nerves drawn taut so long that she'd almost forgotten now to relax. She moved through the conference room and out the long doors into the garden. "Hodarzu, time to come in, baby." When there was no answer, she called again, louder this time, "Hodarzu!"

The garden was empty. A little worried, but not greatly troubled, she went back through the house, calling her son. No answer. She pushed open the front door, frowning. If he was here, he was going to get his bottom spanked. She didn't want him playing around the Mother Well. She walked to the edge of the porch and looked around.

The wilding children were flitting about the courtyard like ragged brown leaves in an eerily silent game of tag that looked more like a wild witch dance than any child's game. And Hodarzu was running with them. The courtyard was filled with snippets of silent laughter and good-natured taunting. They touched and leaped apart following rules she couldn't understand.

"Ah no. Ah no. Ah no. No!" Radiating FEAR, HORROR, ANGER, Kitosime stumbled down the stairs reaching for her son. "No. You won't be wild. Noooo. . . ." Her foot caught in the hem of the dresscloth and she fell headlong on the tiles.

For a moment shock paralyzed her, then she scrambled frantically to her feet and searched for her son.

The children had stopped their game, turned to face her briefly, mouths open in silent screams. As she fell, they wheeled and fled through the arch. Hodarzu fled with them. Kitosime ran to the arch, limping and awkward from the developing pain in her body. She stood rigid in the arch staring out at the silent empty fields, drowning in pain and fear, not her own fear alone, but the memory of the children's fear, of her own son's fear.

She walked heavily to the steps and sat down, looking slowly and blindly around. *My fault,* she thought. *My own stupid fault. I drove them off. Hodarzu.* . . . She was too shocked to cry.

A small hand touched her arm. She stiffened then lifted her head. S'kiliza stood beside her, indigo eyes troubled. She patted Kitosime's arm again and projected COMFORT. Then she pulled Hodarzu from behind her and pushed him toward Kitosime.

The small boy looked hesitantly at Kitosime, reaching toward her, whimpering. She swept him up and hugged him to her, radiating her joy. He snuggled against her, hiding his tear-stained face in the folds of her dresscloth. Then the wilding children were all around her, patting her, projecting their silent laughter, small dirty hands touching her repeatedly until she was the center of a whirlwind of emotion, sharing for a fragile moment their swift, free communion.

She laughed aloud and jumped to her feet, running into the center of the courtyard, still holding Hodarzu in her arms. She danced, wheeling around the Mother Well, the children wheeling and dancing with her. She felt freer than she could remember, the euphoria breaking through the rigid controls she held on her mind and body, so that for a brief time she was projecting and receiving, merging with the group in a flow of love and joy and hope and satisfaction that made nonsense of separate bodies, merging all in the sheer joy of unthinking physical movement.

But the barriers would not stay down. Panting, still laughing, relaxed until her muscles felt soft as cheese and even her bones felt warm inside, she hefted Hodarzu onto her shoulder and strolled toward the house.

At the stairs she felt a puzzling aura of expectancy building behind her. Hodarzu wriggled in her arms. "Down," he demanded. She let him slide to the steps and turned to face the children.

They were standing by the Mother Well. Amea, Wame, S'kiliza. As she watched a strange boy came through the arch, hesitated, then walked to the Well. Two other children followed him, a small scowling boy and a girl.

Kitosime smiled. "Be welcome, children."

The sense of expectancy increased. Six sets of eyes were on her, waiting for something to happen, asking her to do something.

"I don't understand."

S'kiliza projected IMPATIENCE. She jerked Wame in front of her then dropped crosslegged on the tiles. She pantomimed holding something up then shook her finger at Wame. He shuffled, projected PUZZLEMENT over his glee. She shook her finger again. He projected UNDERSTANDING, then walked around to stand beside her facing the others. S'kiliza jumped to her feet and grinned at Kitosime.

Kitosime nodded. "Come here, little one." When S'kiliza came to her, she hugged her and said, "You'll have to help me." She looked over the girl's head toward the mountains. *When you come back I'll have a thing or two to show you, Manoreh my husband.* Aloud she said, "All right, we try. Amea, come here."

The boy hesitated then came to her. The other three started to follow. Kitosime pushed S'kiliza forward. "Make them wait till they're called." When S'kiliza looked puzzled, she pushed her hands forward repeatedly as if she were pushing the new wildings back. She pointed at the three and Wame and pushed again. S'kiliza's thin face lit up and she nodded. She pulled Amea back with her and stood proudly glaring at the newcomers.

"Amea," Kitosime called again. The boy grinned and trotted over to stand beside her. S'kiliza and Wame stopped the others before they could move.

"Wame." He gave a last look at the new ones and joined Amea.

"S'kiliza." The girl came smiling to Kitosime and slid her hand into the older woman's.

A ceremony of naming, Kitosime thought. *A rite for rejoining an abandoned world.* She trembled with a vision of the future, of reclaiming more and more of the wildings. Sighing, she let her eyes move over the three new children.

Two boys and a girl. The tallest and oldest of the boys looked as shy and wary as the spotted chul cat. She pointed a finger at him. "Cheo. Your name will be Cheo." She turned to the smaller boy. His left hand was curled crookedly with a long braided scar curving up from his thumb to a great gouge out of his shoulder muscle. He had a closed, cold look, not quite hostile now. He was waiting, judging. "Liado." She tried to put all the warmth and acceptance she could in her voice. "Your name is Liado."

The wilding girl stood very straight, looking back at her with an odd combination of yearning and hostility. The yearning intensified as her dark eyes glanced at S'kiliza leaning against Kitosime, her head pressed into the curve of Kitosime's hip.

Kitosime smiled at her. "Mara," she said. "You are Mara."

As before, she went around the circle and named them again and again, evoking no spark of understanding in the blank animal eyes watching her. Her hand continued to move, pointing to one after the other as she named them. Finally she stopped and looked at them. They were beginning to smudge into shadow as the sunset colors faded from the sky. "Well," she said. "We try now. Cheo," she called. "Cheo, come here."

None of the wildings moved. S'kiliza stirred impatiently. A small growling sound burst from her. Kitosime looked down, startled. "So you really can speak," she whispered. "Meme Kalamah grant, you'll be talking again." She closed her eyes a moment, trying to hold on to a measure of calm. Then she called again, "Cheo, come here."

She could feel S'kiliza dancing impatiently beside her. Wame pressed into her other side, jiggling nervously, projecting IMPATIENCE at the new ones. Kitosime noted with some surprise that neither was projecting any kind of summoning—another indication of the importance of this ceremony to them. Amea was less passionately involved. He was sitting on the top step waiting patiently for the thing to end.

"Cheo," she called as a pair of almost synchronized *Che's* sounded from the children beside her. "Cheo, come," she called once more, echoed on each side by the children, "Che' co'."

The boy took a hesitant step forward. S'kiliza and Wame vibrated with excitement. Then he walked over to them. Kitosime smiled at him. She reached out. He winced away from her hand, but stood quiet as she smoothed her palm down his cheek and onto his shoulder, a gentle caress that matched the smile on her face and the GLADNESS she was projecting. Then he walked around her and went to sit beside Amea on the top step.

Kitosime fixed her eyes on the small boy. "Liado," she said quietly. "Come here."

" 'Ado co', 'Ado co', 'Ado co'." The two children were jumping up and down excitedly, echoing her, speaking more easily now.

The boy broke suddenly and ran to her, burying his head against her, shaking all over. She stroked gently the matted, greasy hair, saying his name softly over and over until his shuddering stopped. Then he pulled away and went to stand silently beside Wame.

Mara stood drowned in shadow, a lonely, wary figure. Kitosime tightened her lips, annoyed at herself and at the conditioning that made her put the boys first without thinking. She saw Mara wince and move back, hurt by the emotion but unwilling to run out alone into the darkness. Kitosime projected WARMTH as best she could. She waited until Mara stopped moving about then called, "Mara, come here."

She heard giggling on each side and "Mar' co', Mar' co'."

Mara walked with slow pride toward them. Kitosime could feel her urgency and appreciate the self-control it took not to break and run like Liado. She could also see the remnants of Bighouse training and wondered how the child had escaped. Her need must have been terrible. Mara stopped in front of her. Kitosime extended her hand, palm up. Mara laid her palm on it. "Be welcome, sister," Kitosime said quietly. "You honor my house."

Mara recognized the sounds and smiled shyly. Kitosime felt the small hand trembling on hers. She held out her arms. Mara came into them, pressing her body against Kitosime's, shaking as badly as Liado, weeping and fearful and filled with a tentative joy.

When Mara had quieted, Kitosime worked herself free and walked tiredly up the stairs onto the porch with the six wildings and a silent Hodarzu trailing behind her. As she pushed open the front door, she wondered how her soup was doing. *Looks like I'll need it and the bread and cheese too.*

The new wildings hesitated at the door. Kitosime smiled at

them and kicked the wedge in place. "Don't worry, little ones. You can come and go as you will." S'kiliza giggled and ran to the door. She tugged at it to show the others how it would stay open.

When the children had been washed, fed the thick savory soup whose taste made Kitosime smile with pride, along with the bread and cheese, and finally coaxed to bed in the dormitory, Hodarzu with them, Kitosime began to relax. She was still too keyed up to sleep, so she climbed the Manstairs to the roofwalk.

The moonring was in its narrow phase, not giving much light. She looked out over the plain and again felt the quiet pleasure in being alone. She sat down behind the railing, leaning back against one of the shrine posts. The night breeze coiled around her, touching her with a pleasant coolness. Wisps of clouds were blowing across the sky and beginning to pile up. *A storm tomorrow,* she thought. *Or late tonight.*

She felt a stirring on her breast. With an exclamation of disgust she slapped at herself, then gasped in surprise. Not a bug. The eyestones were moving in the neck pouch. She'd forgotten them. She closed her hand over the pouch and felt a warmth through the thin leather. The wind blew colder over her. She crackled with energy, could feel small snappings where her hair touched the shrine behind her. Then the power slipped out of her and she was only tired and a little frightened. Hastily she jumped to her feet and hurried down the stairs to her room.

The watuk grunted and swung over the top of the gate, ignoring the glass shards that tore at his flesh. He hung for a moment, blood sliding down his arms. Face set in a snarl, eyes glazed, breath rasping between his teeth, he was anesthetized by the fury of his blindrage. He dropped, falling badly. One leg buckled under him. Again he ignored the pain as he pushed up and limped to the counterweight. He set bloody palms on the stone and shoved. The gate slammed open and the mob surged in, its silence broken now by growls and wordless roars.

The silence and emptiness of the courtyard defeated them temporarily. They milled about, searching for something to vent their rage on. Then one watuk howled and ran at the Tembeat building. He swung an ax against the great front door, sinking the blade several inches into the wood. He

jerked it loose and swung again. With an ululating growl the
watuk mob converged on the building, breaking in the windows, wrenching off shutters, pouring inside to carry on their
destruction. They tore down hangings, threw books in piles
on the floor, tossed on armloads of clothing and anything else
flammable they could lay hands on, then they set fire to these
piles.

The Director watched the black, oily smoke coil out the
broken windows and shivered at the howling. *Animals,* he
thought. He glanced down the length of the stable loft. *Six
men. Seven, counting me. Not enough. Not near enough.* The
stable was a strong solid building, a good place to defend
with its thick walls and the slit windows lined down one side.
He checked his rifle again, leaned it against the wall, then
tucked the spare ammunition into a neat pile beside the butt.
He looked at his teachers. Six men reclaimed from the wild.
Sheltered here because they had no place outside. Saved from
Fa-fires to be torn apart by a mob of bigots in blindrage. For
a moment he felt a useless old man. He closed his eyes, sunk
in a black depression that sucked out his strength. He was
old, far too old. Old and futile.

Then he thought of the boys hiding somewhere in the
Chwereva complex behind him. And the Rangers Zart, Adel-
eneh and Surin still out mapping and exploring the land on the
far side of the Jinolimas. And Faiseh and Manoreh. He chuckled softly. That thick-head Dallan hadn't understood what
Manoreh was after. His need to swallow the ghost was real, but
he used it to get out of Kiwanji with a groundcar in spite of
the general prohibition, used it to put his nose on Haribu's
trail. The old man wished them luck, hoped the Hunters
would prove as good as men said they were. *Six teachers and
one old legend.* He laughed aloud, drawing surprised looks
from the others. He didn't bother trying to explain. *An old
legend.* They all sang his songs, told wild tales of his achieve-
ments. And forgot him entirely. Angaleh the wanderer. Poet
and maker of songs. A disturber of the peace better pushed
into myth where he couldn't prick people into questioning the
basic assumptions of this society. Now he was the Director.
After twenty years he'd almost forgotten who he was once.
No one had called him by name in all those years. And now
he was going to die. *I'd rather be out with Manoreh,* he
thought. *But so it goes.*

Agoteh shouted and leveled his rifle. As the shot echoed in

the long narrow room, the Director peered out his slit and saw a watuk dropping on his face. Then others came shrieking and howling around the corner. He caught up his rifle and began firing into the mob.

By tens they fell as they ran at the stables. But seven men were not enough. Other tens reached the stable, used their axes on the door, ax handles on the window bars.

The Director heard them pouring in, felt the slam of their hate and rage. He waited for them to swarm up the ladder, laughing again, his old eyes dancing. *A damn good life, mine*, he thought. *Better than any of those bastards can boast*. He shot the first man up the ladder and the second.

He died hard. Like the roots of a water tree, the roots of his life went deep in the wiry old body. He lasted longer than the other teachers. When they were dead, he was still fighting, roaring out his old songs, nearly buried by dead men. But in the end he died. Torn apart by the mob. They worried at him like wild dogs worry their prey. Then they burned the building down around his fragmented body. And wandered back into the street, the blindrage appeased by blood and destruction. With tired satisfaction the attackers left the burning buildings behind them and ambled back to their families for food and sleep.

Grey sat up, conscious at first only of the pain in his body. He grunted as he probed the sorest spots, then grimaced in reluctant appreciation. A delicate job of battering. Every inch of skin bruised and not a bone broken.

Faiseh lay huddled beside him, still out. Grey ran fingers over his head wondering if the watuk had a concussion. There was a knot over his left ear but he was breathing easily. Grey touched the large artery in his neck. A good strong pulse.

Groaning, stretching, working his hands and his body to warm out the stiffness, he walked around their odd prison. They were in a cage six meters on a side with a solid metal sheet underfoot and overhead, joined by heavy square bars about a hand's width apart. He looked through at the room beyond.

They were in a great natural cavern tailored for human usage by slabs of metacrete. At his left a metacrete sheet blocked off part of the cavern. It was pierced by several arches. Through one he could see a gray-floored corridor.

Through another, the obligatory white tiles and complex instrumentation of a lab, with white-coated acolytes bustling about or hovering anxiously over banks of dials. Grey scowled and rubbed at his ribs. These attendants seemed absurdly out of place in the rugged stone of the cavern.

Closer at hand, almost within reach of the cage, a watuk sat crosslegged on a cushion, facing a glass wall with a great maze of glass cubes behind it. Each cube held a limp hare, bulging head shaved, tubes weaving through and around its lumpy body like a glassy cocoon, shimmering lines of force flowing around and over each obscene pink head. Grey counted the cubes. Twenty up, forty across. And behind the front tier, stretching away like fading images in a hazy mirror, more hares, more cubes. He licked his lips, feeling nauseated. Hastily he looked back at the silent, seated watuk.

The watuk's head was shaved and a web of light like those shimmering over the harebrains hovered over it, linked to a polished steel scull cap. Beside him a metal egg a meter and a half tall rested enigmatically on a squat metal cylinder. Man and egg sat on a platform about a meter high, a narrow oval with the long diameter parallel to the harewall. Grey considered the egg thoughtfully. *That has to be the controller,* he thought. *And it can be operated by anyone wearing the cap, looks like.* Aleytys was still loose, coming toward him. Not for long probably. He grinned at the egg, a mirthless stretching of his lips that matched the predator's gleam in his eyes. *Bringing her here, my friend. . . .* He looked around the empty room again, wondering where the thin man was. *Could be the mistake that breaks you.* He thought back to Maeve and the climax of that Hunt, saw Aleytys spinning sunlight into thread and weaving it into a blanket that seared the struggling parasite to ash. *I hope.*

He tapped at his waist where the weapon belt had been and smiled. The belt was a convenience and held some useful things, but its strongest weapon was intangible, existing only in the minds of those who removed it thinking they were disarming him. The belt was a magician's right hand making fancy passes while the plebian left performed the trick. Within his body he had his major weapons, the biologic implants. Small in power but tremendously flexible when supported by his training, experience and that gift of Wolff, his fierce drive for survival.

On the fourth wall outside there was a mosaic screen showing assorted scenes from Kiwanji. He saw the storming of the Tembeat, the fights in the streets, images of the hares silently staring in at the trapped people, images of the generators straining under the load. Grey watched dourly, his professional pride taking a beating. *I'm supposed to be stopping that*, he thought. He shook his head, wondering how the Holders could justify their prohibition of energy weapons. Hundreds of people needlessly dead. *Stupid. Dead because of a damned crazy idea. A twist in the heads of the men in power. Better dead than contaminated by forbidden things. Stupid.* He growled, then burst out laughing. *Getting as bad as Aleytys*, he thought. *None of my business.*

Ignoring the dull ache of his body, he began examining the cage. He ran exploring fingers over the bars, wet the metal with saliva and touched it. Good grade steel. Nothing more. The minitorch in his weaponbelt would cut through them like butter. If he had his weaponbelt. With a degree of privacy and enough time, and one of his implants, he could start a resonance in the metal that would turn it brittle enough to push aside with a flick of his hand. But that would be noisy and lengthy and he was too visible. He touched the heavy welds and paced the circumference of the square. The cage was a quick, neat job, adequate for its purpose, but obviously constructed for the Ranger and for him. He glanced down at Faiseh, frowned. Still out. Then he shrugged. Nothing he could do.

He rubbed his nose. *Which brings up a point. Why am I still alive?*

The cage door was a meter square and located in the far corner of the cage. He knelt beside the door and probed the smooth metal of the lock for the pattern. *A nice job*, he thought. He was still teasing out the pattern when Faiseh groaned and sat up. "Well." He raised his eyebrows. "Took your time."

Faiseh probed at his skull with short blunt fingers. "Feels like I was kicked in the head. And the bastard's still kicking." He squinted at the cage, slowly taking in the sections of the great cavern. "What the hell?"

"Haribu's little home. I think that's what's making the hares attack." He flicked a hand at the egg then swung it at the harewall. "Kiwanji's not wearing too well." He showed Faiseh the mosaic screen.

Faiseh winced as he watched the Tembeat burning. "Meme Kalamah," he whispered. "Everything going . . . ah. . . ."

He edged around and pressed his face against the bars, staring fascinated and horrified at the scenes of disintegration in Kiwanji.

Grey watched a moment then went back to work on the lock. He was unwilling to use his implants when outsiders were watching unless he had to. Sorry about Faiseh's distress, he was satisfied to see him distracted.

Several minutes later Grey grinned and moved away from the lock. Two minutes and he'd be out. His head was still throbbing, made it difficult to work. He wasted a minute cursing the thin man, then triggered his depth probe and began to work out the interior arrangement of Haribu's base. It was like a blind man feeling his way through an unfamiliar house, slowly building up a tactile image. When he had the geography in place, he switched to a heat probe, looking for people. But the hares were a problem. Too close and too many of them. They confused his readings. After a minute he gave up, lounging against the bars.

Faiseh had his face pressed against the bars staring at the scenes from Kiwanji. He hadn't moved. Grey sighed. "Ranger." There was no answer. "Faiseh!"

"Huh?" Reluctantly the watuk swung around. "What?"

"Why whip yourself? Nothing you can do about that. Right time comes, we'll stop it here."

"Here!" The watuk jumped to his feet and started prowling about the cage. "Us!" He banged a fist against the bars. "How?"

"Relax. Sit down!" Grey snapped out the order and Faiseh sat, surprising himself with his instant obedience. "Listen. We wait until Haribu brings Aleytys in. And Manoreh, of course. She's the one to knock that out." He pointed at the egg. "We're backup. When the right time comes, I'll get us out of here. Two minutes. If we jump too soon, we'll get kicked in the head and lose the game."

Faiseh muttered, "Hard to wait."

The hours passed. Faiseh brooded, eventually slept, snoring a little. Grey began counting watuk. Not too many around. About fifteen made a point of walking past the cage and staring at him. All armed. Guards. He counted five different white-coated lab workers.

A wizened little man—a tarnished green-silver hard as a dried pea—trotted from the lab, a taller dull-faced watuk behind him. The little man's white coat was starchy, pristine, not a wrinkle marring it even when he moved. Grey leaned forward, watching intently. The strange pair stopped beside the platform.

"Charar!" The little man's voice was sharp and scratchy.

The sitter stirred, slowly straightened his legs. After a minute he eased the cap off his head and set it carefully on a black box beside his cushion. Muscles trembling with fatigue, he rose clumsily and stumbled off the dais, nearly falling on his face. He shambled off saying nothing to the others and disappeared into the gray-floored corridor on the far end of the metacrete wall.

The wizened man glanced at the screen, then urged his companion onto the dais. "Keep them at it," he shrilled. His black-beetle eyes darted from the screen to the sitter and back. "More pressure. We need more pressure. It's taking too long." He watched impatiently as the watuk settled the cap on his shaved head. "Careful. Careful. Get it seated, fool, you mess up and I'll see you hurt for it." His beetle eyes took in the egg. "If I knew more about that or could get a look inside!" He reached out and almost touched the silver-gray surface but stopped his fingers a hair away from it. "Fa curse that Vryhh." He stopped abruptly and looked anxiously around, then turned back to the silent watuk sitting on the cushion. He nodded, then walked briskly away.

Vryhh," Grey whispered. He glanced from the egg to the hares lying in the glass cubes. *The redhead. A Vryhh. Interesting. No wonder he handled me like a baby. Aleytys can't know. This changes things. She's half-Vryhh. Can she handle him? Should be a damn good fight. That answers Head's question. Don't have to wonder how he got to her.*

He pushed his still sore body erect and moved back to where he could see the depressing scenes of Kiwanji as it disintegrated under the pressure of the hares, then faced the harewall. *Crude now,* he thought. He began to think about his own presence here, began to see possibilities that spread and branched until he was near the limits of his imagination. He thought of the hareweapon, refined and increased a thousandfold in power, focused on Wolff. In winter. People pouring out of houses onto the ice. *God! And if . . . no, when they turned that monster on me, everything about Wolff and the Hunters. Too many people, worlds, Companies with reasons for hitting Wolff.*

He felt the Vryhh before he saw him. He looked up. The

man stood outside the cage watching him, green-stone eyes amused and contemptuous. Grey stared back, silently defiant. Legends, these Vrya. Near omniscience. Omnipotence. He glared into the handsome, masklike face, then at the withered hands and their metal inlays. After a minute he smiled. Not a legend. Diseased. Dying. His smile broadened and he lifted his gaze back to the Vryhh's face. The green eyes narrowed and the mask slipped a little as he gave way to irritation. He turned abruptly and stalked off, vanishing into a small lift beside the harewall.

Grey settled back against the bars and stared at the egg. Seeing the Vryhh reminded him of Aleytys. He remembered the first time he'd seen her. He'd been lying in the third-floor corridor of a cheap hotel on Maeve bleeding his life out on the worn carpet, a knife hole big as his fist in his stomach. He could use that healing now. He rubbed at his sore diaphragm. He looked across at the snoring Ranger then settled down and drifted to sleep.

They rode all night, stopped briefly for a cold meal, then went on, following the course of the Chumquivir up into the mountains. Hare traces were abundantly present. Droppings, mangled vegetation. During the night the link pulled them closer and closer until each lived partly in two bodies, sensing what the other sensed. They rode silently, saying nothing, both growing more resentful of this enforced intimacy.

A faras stumbled. Aleytys reacted immediately, shifting her weight to lift the faras, then gasped as pain stabbed through her groin. Her hands opened, the reins fell, her mount reared then started to run. She was falling, no she was sitting clutching the saddle horn jolting helplessly as the faras ran. She set herself to controlling the animal. When she rode back, Manoreh was standing beside a dead faras. One of his legs was braced, the other bent with only the toe touching the ground. She fought against the pain that pierced her own leg and side. "What happened?"

"Leg broke. Cut its throat," he grunted. Aleytys winced again as the pain in his side was a pain in hers.

"Stupid." She pressed her hand against her forehead. "You should have waited."

He ignored her and removed the gear from the dead animal.

Aleytys slid from the saddle. "Let that go a minute. Sit down."

Breathing with difficulty, he tugged a strap loose, then started on another.

"Sulking like a baby." She sneered, "Won't listen to a woman, will you, big man."

He swung around, arm raised for a quick slap, stung to rage by her words.

"Go on, hit me. Prove what a man you are."

He dropped the hand and turned away, sick with self-disgust.

"All right, now that's over. . . ." She touched his arm. The shock of joining staggered both, then Aleytys fought loose. "Sit down," she said hoarsely. She went with him to one of the rock piles that broke the thatching of brush and grass.

He sat and looked up at her. "What's the point?" he said wearily.

She knelt beside him. "I'm a healer, Manoreh. Just sit still and let me work." She closed her eyes and reached for her power river. The black water came cool and powerful into her. She slid the tips of her fingers lightly down his ribs, past the pelvis, then down the injured leg. The strains and bruises located, she flattened her hands against him and sent the water flowing to heal.

When the healing was done, she tried to pull her hands away. Her flesh stuck to his even through the leather of his jerkin and shorts. She took a deep breath, concentrated on the hands flattened over his ribs and over the big muscle of his thigh. She called up her ability to shield and slid a barrier between them. Tried again to lift her hands. This time they slid easily off him.

She met his startled look. "For a moment I couldn't move. Stuck." She looked down at her hands, rubbed them together. "Started to panic."

He stared past her at the horizon. Both could sense Haribu hovering here, chuckling maliciously. Aleytys shuddered. Manoreh shuddered. Both sat silent until the echoes of that laughter passed away and the presence retreated. Then Manoreh straightened. He slid his hand down over his body. "Useful gift."

Aleytys smiled and reached out, then jerked her hand

away. "I'll have to change my habits." Her hand dropped onto her thigh. "Well? What now?"

He glanced at the dead faras. "Looks like I walk. My own fault. I didn't know." He turned back to her. "We can't ride double."

"Very bad idea." She suppressed an urge to laugh, saw him puzzled as he felt her amusement. "We take turns walking," she said firmly.

He started to protest. Then he shrugged. "We're just going through the motions anyway. Haribu can pick us up any time he wants." He looked over the line where the mountain ridge met the sky. "No point in wearing ourselves out."

She did laugh then shook her head. "The best bait wiggles vigorously to attract the prey."

Manoreh snorted. He stood up, looking down at her. "Let's go."

They moved up into the mountains following the river and the scattered piles of hare pellets. Higher and higher into the mountains, with breath coming in short pants and sweat streaming down their faces. Behind them clouds gathered over the Sawasawa but here the sun shone through the thin air and sucked the moisture from their bodies. Lips cracked, noses began to bleed as the membranes dried out.

About midafternoon Aleytys stopped, scowled at the sun, then left the scratch trail and scrambled down the unsteady scree to the narrowing river below. She ducked her head under the water and splashed happily about. After a while she looked up and saw Manoreh squatting beside the water.

"Take a break. Try this." She splashed at him and laughed as he pulled back fastidiously. Even though she was fully clothed, he radiated embarrassment. She lay back and shook her head at him. "I was about to dry up and blow away. You're not much better off, friend." He stood and walked around a bend in the stream. After a few minutes she could hear water splashing. Once again she shook her head. "Dumb," she muttered. Reluctantly she crawled out of the river and climbed cautiously up the rock pile to the patient faras.

Manoreh joined her, water beading on his silver-green scales. Aleytys kicked at a pile of hare pellets. "Hundreds of hares have come along here. Think Haribu's breeding them?"

"Must be." He scanned the mountains tilting up before them. "Why is he waiting?"

"Lazy maybe. Why bother when we're coming on our own? Maybe he just likes tormenting us. What do you think?"

"I think it's your turn to ride."

The shadows were heavy and long when Manoreh put a hand on the faras's shoulder, stopping it. The sky was darkening, a few glowing clouds drifting toward the plain. "He sits there laughing at us." He turned his head to stare toward faraway Kiwanji. After a moment's silence, he muttered, "It must be hell there now. Meme Kalamah! We have to finish this. Haribu! Where the hell are you?"

Aleytys looked around. They were close to water. There was dirt underfoot, a sparse covering of grass, some trees and down wood, and a patch of brush to cut the force of the wind. She slid off the faras. "I'm tired and hungry. Let's stop for the night. This is a good enough place to camp."

Later she sat staring into the coals of their meager fire, sipping at a cup of cha and listening to Manoreh as he splashed about downstream, carefully out of sight. She smiled with amusement and a little affection. He irritated her but he was a good man to have on one's side in a fight. She turned her smile on the fire. It was a game they were playing. A deadly game. Their fire was a shout of defiance to Haribu, a sign telling him they knew he watched.

Manoreh came back holding his jerkin. The faint light from the coals gleamed on his hard, flat chest. Aleytys watched with tired pleasure as he knelt and reached for the hot cha-pot, folding a bit of leather jerkin around the metal handle. He poured a cup then sat down across the fire from her. "Why?"

"Appreciation of male beauty." She chuckled. "I know. Very unfeminine of me."

Then the cha pot was empty and the coals black. Overhead the moonring was a thin scattering of sparks. Manoreh was tidily packing the pots away. He was a careful man on the trail, would be ready to move with a minimum of delay if the need arose. Aleytys lay back and watched him stir about. When he finished spreading his blanket and was preparing to wrap himself for the night, she said, "Do we set watch?"

"Why?" He looked over his shoulder at her. "I'm a fool. Must sleep farther apart. Might help." He watched her a minute then laughed. "Do I move or you?"

Aleytys echoed his amusement. "Since you're already

settled. . . ." She jumped to her feet, carrying her blanket up
with her. Still laughing, she started off around the bend then
stopped and looked up as a dark shadow cut across the
moonring and a whine smothered the night noises. She
glanced back at Manoreh.

He was on his knees, struggling for calm, teetering on the
edge of the watuk blindrage. Then he stood with a stubborn
pride, projecting DEFIANCE at the circling skimmer.

Aleytys reached out with her talent, stroked mind fingers
over the engine. She knew it now, knew its vulnerable places.
She could wreck it in seconds with no more effort than it
took to snap fingers. She glanced at Manoreh. Not the time
for that now. The little fish was nibbling and would take
them to the shark. Then the stun beam hit and there was
nothing.

The Fa-kichwa Gakpeh stood on the rounded top of the
great rock and gazed down on the Sawasawa. The morning's
storm was passing slowly off, uncovering the isolated patches
of green that marked the locations of the Holdings. Behind
him the clouds were beginning to remake and slide down
from the peaks for another storm that would break over the
valley early the next morning. He pulled his chul-fur cloak
about him. The air dropping down over the cliff was damp
and chill. He couldn't tear his eyes away from the land below. There were wildings down there, he knew it, running in
and out of the abandoned houses. They always came once the
hares had cleared the way. The hares. He leaned forward,
peering intently at the gray-green juapepo scum. No white
down there. Hares must all be at Kiwanji. He smiled fiercely.
Let them purge that cursed place. Let it burn and be left
empty. He brooded a while over the land, sick and angry at
the thought of defiling wildings running free over Vodufa
Holdings.

An hour later he was riding down the mountainside with
his company—Sniffer, Second, Fireman and hounds. Riding
toward the nearest Holding.

In Kiwanji the blindrage was stirring again among the watuk males. More and more of them were pacing the rutted
streets around the sides of Chwereva complex, their booted
feet abrading the hard-packed earth, stirring heavy clouds of
red dust as they walked. But even the blindrage wasn't

enough to drive them against those massive walls of machine-cut stone with the energy guns mounted like dark, ugly demons at the four corners of the compound.

The blindrage turned inward, driving watuk against watuk until the street stank with the putrefying bodies of men knifed or beaten to death.

In the shelters the women huddled together trying to endure terror and tension. Some couldn't stand it any longer and went silently to the low stone wall at the psi-screen. They stood staring out at the bulging brown eyes staring relentlessly back at them. For hours they stood. Then slowly, one by one, or in groups of two or three, sometimes holding hands for comfort, they knelt, Bighouse woman and Bound together, caste distinctions buried in their common terror. They touched foreheads to the ground, then stepped silently over the wall, giving themselves to the hares as in other places and other times women driven beyond endurance had danced off cliffs or into the sea.

Inside Chwereva the boys lay hidden still, waiting, eating the trail rations Agoteh had given them and drinking water stolen from the stable taps late at night. Umeme had climbed the wall and looked down into the Tembeat. With a friend waiting at the top of the wall to give warning if any Chwerevaman came around, he went down into the ashes of the stable and flitted through broken shadows into the Tembeat.

He came back filled with a bitter anger and overwhelming grief. At first he couldn't tell them what he'd found, but later that night he did—needing to purge his memories of the horror.

Kitosime dipped the gourd into the dark water and lifted it, holding it above the stone basin, drops falling back in a slowing patter to pock with silver the mirror surface. Overhead the two stone lamps flickered red and gold, breathing a fragrant black mist at the low ceiling already blackened from two centuries of ceremony.

With great concentration she poured the water on the five powerstones, deriving her ceremony from images that welled up from deep inside her, humming intensely a rising and falling tune that came from the same darkness. Her body vibrated with it and it grew stronger and stronger as the stones woke, answering to the names she gave them. Black Wehweli. Agodoz, amber-brown with paler spots. Leghu, green and white like frozen water. And the Twins, both a pale, pale blue. In the half-light of the roof shrine with the storm wheeling in great circles outside, the rain coming in gusts against lowered louvers, lightning turning the darkness white, the power stones hissed under the touch of the water and sang with the power in their pattern. The air shook around her.

The eyestones waited in front of her knees. She felt them waiting. Taut. Desiring. Her body hummed with their desire. She struggled. Sought. The humming clashed, then began merging. She felt it merge. Felt the power coming into her hands, her arms. She lifted the gourd high, then dashed the last of the water on the eyestones. She swayed her upper body as the humming power consumed her. She felt a great heat, saw flickers of red and yellow. Images stirred against the darkness, swung around and around in dizzying circles, around and around, crossing behind her and coming to the front again, blurred glows that sharpened into faces. . . .

Hodarzu's face. Puzzled. Wrinkling to cry.
Fa-men bent over him, assegais dripping red. Blood running, pumping out the spear tips. Changing to smoke figures. Wavering. Fading. Changing. . . .
Manoreh flat on his back, pinned to a table by broad flat straps, naked, head shaved, a web of light obscuring his face.
The Woman. The Hunter woman, red-headed. Standing. Flames leaping out from her like sun rays. Power. Deadly. Killing, power radiating out from her. To touch Manoreh. To enter him and explode outward. . . .
Haribu. Thin horrible creature. Old. Obscenely old. Looking young but old. Green eyes stone-hard. Withering to death, the old man. Evil. Haribu. . . .
Fa-men standing over her. She crouched on a floor holding Hodarzu. Bent over her. Threatening her. Pressing down on her. Fa-men. Fa-men. . . .

Abruptly the humming power was gone, wrenching itself free as waves of need swept across her. She blinked, dazed, struggling to control her own terror awakened by the images, then heard the cries coming from outside.

" 'Tosime! 'Tosime! Mama 'Tosime!" The children's voices

pulled her. Once again her foot caught in the hem and she
stumbled, slamming her head into the door post. For a moment she was paralyzed by the shock, then she fumbled her
way outside and stood blinking into a lightning flash as a gust
of rain caught her in the face.

"You're all soaked! What is it?"

Shielding her eyes from the water streaming down her
face, S'kiliza stared up at her, body shaking with anxiety.
"Mama, come down." She took Kitosime's hand and pulled
her to the stairs. The other children, silent but projecting
their own terror, followed, crowding close against her.

At the stairs she lifted her dresscloth high and fled down-
ward, pushed on by the panic of her children. The big front
door was open. She ran through to the porch, dropping the
cloth as she passed the door. She stopped, smoothing her
dress into place with shaking hands.

An adult wilding stood panting beside the Mother Well,
rain streaming thickly over the ingrained dirt on his face. His
right hand was closed tightly about his left forearm. Blood
welled out between his bony fingers and spattered slowly onto
the court tiles to mix with the film of rain water and spread
into wide, pale smudges of red. He was thin, starved to the
bone, but he gazed at her with a stubborn pride that reminded her for a fleeting instant of Manoreh. She brushed the
thought impatiently aside and turned to Mara. "Mara, there
are clean cloths in the kitchen. Bring them here, would you,
little one?" As the girl ran into the house, Kitosime smiled at
the other children. "Do you think you could persuade your
friend to come up here out of the wet?"

Cheo and Amea nodded eagerly and ran down the steps.
They roared REASSURANCE at the man and began tugging at
his unwounded arm. At first he resisted, his eyes on Kitosime.
She closed her eyes, tried to project WELCOME. She was better at that now. She smiled to think that some day she could
perhaps speak and project with equal fluency. When she
opened her eyes again, he was climbing the steps slowly and
with some difficulty, swaying with his growing weakness, but
he'd lost his fear of her.

Then Mara was back with the cloths. Kitosime tore one of
them into strips and began bandaging the ugly tear in the
muscle of his arm. She glanced over her shoulder at the boys.
"Wame, what's this about? How did this man get hurt?"

The man winced as she spoke. It suddenly occurred to her

that pain explained why wilding children stopped talking. She
shook her head, cursing once again her own ignorance that
kept her fumbling her way to ideas a little more knowledge
would bring to her easily. She tied a careful knot and tucked
the ends of the bandage under, then tugged the man down
until they were both sitting on the floor of the porch. She
tilted her head up at Wame, waiting.

The small boy straightened his body proudly. He had a gift
for story telling and apparently wanted to make up for years
of silence in a few days for he was always chattering. He
grinned at the wilding, then sobered, remembering the fright-
ful things he had to tell. "Fa-men," he said. "Come down out
of the mountains now the hares are gone." He swept his hand
in a wide arc from north to south. "Holdings are empty. The
wildings, they come out of the juapepo." He pantomimed a
wary looking about, then a joyful dance, hands gathering invisible treasures to himself. "They need much. They have
hunger. They are naked." He pointed at the dirty hide about
the adult wilding's loins. "They remember the good ways of
their fathers who have denied them. They remember and are
sad. Now they come and take. They are clean and not hungry for a little while. The hares chase the Fa-men away. Now
the Fa-men they come back. They take wildings to burn and
eat. They know the hares are all at Kiwanji. They do not fear
the hares. They send the hounds after the wildings. They cut
with assegais. They put ropes on wilding necks. They make a
great fire and burn them. Then they eat them and drink their
blood. This man he run from them. They follow him. The
hounds sniff for him. He run past here. He FEEL us. He come
in to warn us. Fa-men come here soon." Wame shivered as
the wind blew a scattering of raindrops onto the porch. "The
rain, it help. Hide him from the hounds. But look." He
pointed to a thinning patch of cloud where the storm was
beginning to break up. "They come to all Holdings." He held
up a hand, thumb and forefinger about two centimeters apart.
"About this much time before they are here. This one, he tell
us to run now while the rain hide our scent. He want to leave
now."

Kitosime wiped the damp from her face. She smiled at the
wilding and tried to project REASSURANCE/UNDERSTANDING.

He touched her cheek with the tips of his fingers, projected
GLADNESS/WARNING/QUESTION?

A hand touched Kitosime's shoulder. She looked up. Cheo. He held a sack, and thrust it at her, projecting QUESTION?

She took it, felt the round hardness inside and laughed, projected PRIDE! As the boy shuffled back, embarrassed, she put the sack on the wilding's knee. She opened it, let him see the golden-brown loaves inside, then pulled the neck strings tight and closed his fingers around them.

He touched her arm, got heavily to his feet, then trotted down the steps, splashed across the courtyard. At the arch he hesitated and looked back, projected WARNING!! then vanished into the gray rain. It was still coming down hard enough to wash out his scent and erase what marks he made. Kitosime got to her feet. "He's got a good chance," she told the children. S'kiliza pressed against her, trembling and uncertain. Liado and the others crowded around her too, even the big boys. Liado was on the verge of hysteria. He'd felt Fa-hound's teeth and only escaped by falling into the river and nearly drowning. She held him tight against her. "I promise. I won't let them get you. I promise you."

Then she worked free of the clinging children and said briskly, "And if I want to keep that promise, we'd all better get busy."

Aleytys sneezed. Stale dust tickled into her nose. She was piled in a heap, face down on a rug, her body one great ache. She rolled over and straightened her legs, eyes still tight shut, then reached out for the black river and slammed against the restraint of an inhibitor. "Shit!" She ground the heels of her hands into her eyes. "Not again. Can't they ever think of something else?"

She grimaced. There was a harsh metallic taste in her mouth. A sudden soft whoosh of air stilled her body. The whisper of feet moved over the deep rug, then there was a presence standing over her. She continued to lie still, her eyes shut, breathing steadily. The footsteps whispered away again. She heard more faint noises, then they stopped. *Sitting,* she thought. *Probably watching me.*

She ignored the presence and returned to sorting out her sensations. Mouth dry. Slow rolls of nausea. Numbness in the tips of her fingers. That taste in the mouth. Babble drug. *Leukoy or mequat.* She forced herself to relax. *Next year,* she thought. *Next year I get my conditioning. Now . . . now he knows everything he had the wits to ask for.*

She began poking at the limits allowed her by the inhibitor. The claustrophobia induced by the walls around her mind stirred up the settling nausea in her stomach. She swallowed. Then she remembered Manoreh. *The link. What about the link?* As his image strengthened in her mind, she became aware of him. When she concentrated she felt pressure on her ankles and wrists and a lighter pressure across thighs, waist and shoulders. *Bound to a flat surface wherever he was.* Briefly she wondered why the inhibitor hadn't cut the link. Maybe a matter of sheer power. Forgetting to remain passive, she rubbed at a warm spot under her collarbone without thinking of what it meant. *Haribu. Wonder if that's him watching me. . . .*

Then she realized what she was doing and what that warm spot should have told her. Grey! Here too. Sudden terror brought her sitting upright, staring at the foot of a wide bed. Her backup was taken out before the game began. She pushed the tumbled hair out of her face and forced down her rising panic. She sucked in a deep breath, then swung quietly around to face the man sitting in the pneumochair watching her.

Metal clinked. Her thigh brushed something cold. She looked down, realizing for the first time that she was naked. She laughed and fingered the cuffed chain beside her, then leaned back against the bed and gurgled with amusement. "How melodramatic." The absurdity of the situation struck her as she examined her captor.

A long man, grotesquely thin. The hands resting lightly on the chair arm were plated with metal. Exoskeleton. Narrow triangular face. Parchment skin crossed and recrossed by thousands of tiny wrinkles. Hair as red as hers and cold green eyes.

She pulled fingers through the tangled strands of her hair. Her nudity didn't bother her nearly as much as her untidy hair. For some reason he'd undone her braids but hadn't bothered to comb the hair out. She touched a sore spot at the base of her skull. She poked gently at the lump, a slight swelling around the neck bones.

The man in the chair spoke quietly. "Tampering with the inhibitor will cause a small explosion that will blow your head off your shoulders, Hunter."

"I see." She let her hand fall, moved her head tentatively back and forth. "A little stiff."

"You'll get used to it."

"You're Vryhh." She frowned. "Haribu? Isn't this a bit small for a Vryhh?"

The Vryhh smiled but the curling of his lips left his eyes dull green like filmed jade. "Not small, halfling. Not for the RMoahl diadem."

"Ah!" Involuntarily she touched her temple. "Did you enjoy your stroll through my head, Vryhh?"

His smile widened and the green eyes began to glint with malice. "I wonder how far Vryhh traits breed true. Shall we stop by the vadi Kard and take a look at your son?"

Aleytys's mouth went dry. She watched the narrow cat face of the Vryhh, the cold eyes feeding on her pain. "No." She leaned against the bed and swallowed further protest. "You were the one with the Chwereva in Head's office. You were the one who tampered with her mind. For the diadem?"

"In part. It's unique."

"Hah! Why am I still alive? Now that I know what you're after, I don't mean to make an easy corpse."

He was briefly amused. "Corpse?" He came out of the chair gracefully, the exoskeleton a marvel of engineering. When he reached her, he bent down and touched her hair with his fingertips, then tapped lightly at her temples. His face was so close she could track the thousands of tiny lines in his skin. "I'm Vryhh, not some halfwit RMoahl. I know how to purge the diadem out of you and leave you alive to enjoy the other things I've planned for you." He was coldly amused by her involuntary grimace of distaste.

Aleytys rubbed at her nose. "You're very thorough. Mequat or leukoy?"

He ignored her questions, stared down at her, his pale face filled with scorn. Then there was a sudden hot glare in his eyes, his mouth twisted, and he spat in her face. He hauled her to her feet and threw her away, suddenly, violently slamming her against the wall.

She screamed. When she collapsed on the floor, he was beside her, jerking her back to her feet. He slapped her into silence, the metal on his hands cutting into her skin and cracking the bone of her jaw. "Shereem's get," he hissed. "Halfblood. Mud! I'll parade you before them after I'm done with you and they'll see her rotten. . . ." He hissed in fury.

Horrified at the madness in his face, confused by the pain

in her head and body, she hung in his hands thinking, *he hates her. Hates my mother. Crazy. . . .*

He dropped her and strode away. While she struggled onto her knees, he settled himself in the pneumochair and watched her. After a minute he turned back a sleeve, exposing a long, narrow plate with two rows of touch-sensors. He flicked his fingers in a rapid pattern over the sensors. When he looked up, she felt the clamp gone from her head. "Heal yourself, mud," he snarled.

Forcing tears from under shut eyelids in her agony, Aleytys wove a fine force web to pull her broken jaw into place, then reached for the black river. The cool, cool water flowed into her, washing away the pain, healing the breaks and the bruises. As her strength returned, she glanced at the Vryhh. He was watching her intently, fingers ready on the arm wearing the sensor plate. *Not yet,* she thought. *But I know one of his weaknesses now.* As the water flowed away, she trapped a great pool of it within herself. Then she felt the inhibitor clamp down again.

The powerpool began to seethe and surge at the restraints she held around it. She had a sense of extreme danger. Fighting to hold it stable, she sat very still, watching the Vryhh. For several long minutes they stared at each other, Vryhh and half-Vryhh. Then he came out of the chair again and pointed at the wall beside her. A door slid back.

"Stand up, mud," he said softly.

Aleytys pushed onto her feet and waited.

"Come here, mud."

Watching his hands, she walked slowly to his side. The room, now visible, was a fresher with a cleansing cabinet and a toilet. A small prison of a room, harsh and unlovely. The Vryhh's hand came down on her shoulder. She suppressed a shudder at the dry papery feel of his skin. His touch made her feel unclean, as if by simple contact he could taint her with his disease. "Wash yourself, mud," he whispered. He played with her hair, then pushed her inside.

When she came out, he was back in the chair, a length of shimmering cloth spread over his legs. She stopped, waiting for him to speak.

"Come here." He lifted the length of velvet, dark green with a bluish tinge in the shadows and silver where the pile caught the light.

She took the dress, careful not to touch his hands. The thought of touching him again nauseated her.

"Put it on." There was an odd light in his eyes, a caress in his rich dark voice.

Aleytys looked at the soft material in her hands, more frightened by the new softness in his voice than she'd been by his violence. Madness. She thought wistfully of Harskari. "I need you, Mother," she whispered, but there was no answer. *What this new turn means . . . God, I can't understand him. How can I deal with craziness?* She slid the dress over her head and smoothed it down. *Wait and see.* She caught the brush he threw at her and began to work on her hair.

He looked her over when she was finished. Her hair was brushed to a silk firefall hanging halfway down her back. The velvet clung to her breasts and hips and swung in long graceful folds around her ankles, changing color in ripples when she shifted from foot to foot. She stiffened as he slid out of the chair and came toward her. He fastened a fine gold chain around her neck, the pendant gem glowing with green fire against her skin in the deep scoop neck of the dress. He then slipped a matching ring onto her finger.

He stepped back and ran his eyes over her. "Straighten your shoulders, halfling. Hold your head up." His deep voice was still caressing her. He stroked withered fingers down the side of her face. "Vryhh skin," he murmured. His fingers slipped under her chin and jerked her head up. "But the wrong color, halfling." His face swam in her vision. From a great distance she heard the soft voice. "No, that's too easy."

He threw her away again, the exoskeleton driving her up and back in a tumble of arms and legs. This time she landed on the bed, sprawled ungracefully, the dress hiked up about her waist, her stomach jerking with nausea. She sat up, smoothing her hair back and pulling her dress down.

"One of these times you'll break my neck." She stroked exploring fingers over the new bruises on her throat. "What do you want of me?"

"Halfling." He smiled. "Silence. Cooperation. You belong to me, blood of my blood, kinswoman. I'm Kell of Tennath, halfling, Tennath himself. Word of a Vryhh, you'll live a long, long time with me. As will your son."

"You seem fascinated by my half-blood." She ran cold eyes over his body. "I suppose your appetites are as diseased as your form."

His eyes went briefly venomous, then filmed over until they were blank and flat as green stone. "Judge for yourself."

"Not if I can help it."

"Can you help it, halfling?"

"I can damn well try."

"Will you, halfling?" He came to the bed and sat beside her. He touched the curve of her neck, then stroked his dry fingertips up and down the flesh until she was shivering with disgust and fear. His hands moved over her body, nothing tender at all in the harsh probing that meant only that he was master of her flesh, able to use it however he wanted. Then he pushed her backwards until she sprawled once again on the bed. "I have your associate in a cage, Hunter. I was going to take you down and show you my little zoo. I've changed my mind. I'll wait till we're ready to use the hares on him. Interesting to see how long it takes Dr. Songoa to break his conditioning."

She pushed the hair out of her face. "Too bored to do it yourself?"

He laughed and walked away, disappearing through a sudden door in the far wall, leaving her lying on the bed more confused than ever. According to the reports she'd read, one of the effects of his disease was impotence. Whether that was true for a Vryhh, she didn't know. His actions indicated otherwise, but that might be pride. Disgusted, she sat up. She pulled the dress over her head, tossed it down beside the bed and threw the jewelry after it. Then she stretched out on the bed, hands laced behind her head. *Wait and see,* she thought. She even found a measure of pity for the man who claimed kinship with her. Arrogant, with an extended lifespan, accustomed to physical beauty, what was he now? She shivered and wrenched her mind from these profitless speculations and began probing once again at the limitations of the inhibitor.

She reached Manoreh. He was raging wildly at something that absorbed his whole attention. His rage flooded her, tied her temporarily in knots. She struggled to push it away without having to withdraw from the link. Her interference distracted him. He broke from the blindrage and projected SURPRISE along the link, then a sudden burst of understanding. . . .

There was a slow rising out of blackness into a throbbing

pain that took over his head. For a moment Manoreh floated, lost, unable to remember who or what he was. Then the memory of the night camp came back. The skimmer. The stunbeam. He tried to sit up but he was bound to something. Straining against the ache that started at the base of his skull and climbed over his ears to his temples, he arched his neck and looked along his body.

Broad straps passed over his chest and pelvic area. Two straps pinned each of his arms and others crossed each thigh, calf and ankle. He dropped his head back and felt the metal cap that curved over it pressing into his flesh.

A watuk in a white coat swam into view, bent over him, pulled at the straps. Then he went away. Manoreh turned his head from side to side. He was in some kind of laboratory. He could see several of the white-coated workers bustling about as they had in the secret books the Director had made them read. The first man came back and began fussing with the thing on the Ranger's head. "What's happening?" Manoreh turned his head.

The man clucked disapproval and forced it back, ignoring Manoreh's words as a man would ignore the squeaks and growls of an experimental animal.

Another face floated over him. A familiar face. Grinning with malice. Manoreh's hands closed into fists that beat futilely at the padded surface of the table that held him. Testre Dallan. He stared up into the weakly triumphant face, intending to say nothing but the rage betrayed him. "Traitor," he spat. "May your body rot until it matches the stink of your soul."

Dallen jerked back, sweating. He wheeled to face someone out of Manoreh's range of vision. "Kill him, the freak, he's dangerous."

"Don't be a fool." The dark rich voice startled Manoreh then he felt the touch that was all too familiar.

"Haribu," he breathed. He struggled to move his head around to see his enemy. But the neckband limited his movement too much. Once again the blindrage took him and he fought against his bonds until a questing touch startled him out of his mindless struggle. Another familiar touch. Aleytys. The link between them was still in place. He was faintly surprised, then he understood. She was a prisoner too. She felt his pain, and sent a little power down the link and his pain was gone. He shut his lips over a shout of triumph.

Dallan fidgeted about, moving in and out of Manoreh's sight. Behind him Haribu and a watuk he called Dr. Songoa were talking.

"You have your subject, Songoa. One of the empaths this world has produced. What are you going to try first?"

Songoa sniffed. "First we try sheer power, building in measured increments to see if we can crush the Ranger's resistance." He peered at the dials on one of the instruments. "The readings on him are a bit surprising." He walked past Dallan, totally ignoring the nervous watuk. Stopping beside Manoreh, he probed at the skullcap then poked at Manoreh's ribs. His head jerked on a long thin neck, his small round eyes glittered with anticipation. "Several anomalies. Inflow of activity from some outside source, might be. Hard to say." His small, pouty mouth stretched into a mirthless grin. "You can't fool us, Ranger. We'll find out all your little secrets."

"What if he doesn't break?" The speaker moved into view, a narrow red-headed man. Haribu, Manoreh thought.

"That seems unlikely. However it's all information, whatever happens. Useful." He sniffed again. "We have other experiments set up. Almost hope he holds. Get more information that way." He walked away. Manoreh turned his head, following the wizened little watuk's move to the instrument bank. With a sticklike finger, Songoa tapped a sensor. "We begin." He fussed over his panel, dark eyes darting from one readout to another with the bright alertness of a bird.

Manoreh jerked his head straight, forgetting about Haribu and Dallan as pressure clamped down around his head as if a thousand wires were being twisted tighter and tighter. His body arched under the straps as he fought back, pushing outward, trying to drive the sensation away. He set himself to resist. Resist! It grew. Breathing was hard. The air was dead. He was being squeezed. Squeezed down to nothing. Nothing.

Through the link, like a distant memory too fuzzy to identify, he felt Aleytys tremble and fumble for coherent thought. She suffered with him and she felt him failing under the pressure and he felt a touch of shame for her to see him so weak. And felt her acceptance and affection. He could feel her soft fingers touching him. He was failing. The pressure was too much. She reached through the link to help him. The trickle of power down the link surprised and nearly betrayed him, but he recovered in time and took the energizing pseudo-liquid and used it to drive his defenses. He laughed as the pressure retreated. The doctor began muttering worriedly. Back and back he drove it. The doctor twittered. Back and back. Hastily Songoa tapped fleshless fingers over the sensor plate. Manoreh expelled a puff of air as the pressure relaxed and let his straining body rest. Then he lay smiling quietly.

"What happened?" Haribu sounded impatient. He brushed past Songoa and glanced over the dials.

"Remarkable. Really remarkable. I had no idea."

"What?" Haribu rested his hand on Songoa's shoulder. "What are you babbling about?"

The doctor sniffed, annoyed. He pushed at the hand and refused to answer until it was removed. "Really remarkable. He resisted the force that's breaking Kiwanji down. During that last minute I channeled all power into him, everything, you understand, and if I hadn't reversed, the back pressure would have blown. . . ." He patted the instrument panel, tutting worriedly.

Dallan sidled around Manoreh and stared at the panel. "What now?" he shrilled. "I thought you said you could break him."

Songoa shot him a contemptuous look. Ignoring both men, he turned to the panel and began reprogramming.

Manoreh edged his head around. For some reason Haribu reminded him of Aleytys. The hair, maybe. And something elusive about the face. *Seeing things*, he thought. He sent a glow of appreciation along the link to Aleytys and felt her pleased response. Together they were beating Haribu. Kell, that's what Songoa called him.

Small itches began moving over Manoreh's head. He flashed a warning to Aleytys and settled in to resist this new attack. The itches started at the forehead and ran in successive waves to his neck. It was mildly irritating but nothing like that aching pressure of the first attack. He wondered what was supposed to be happening and moved his body restlessly against the straps to relieve the itch of restlessness. Dallan heard the rustle of his movement and bustled over, satisfaction oily in his little round face.

After several minutes of the successive itch waves, his body was vibrating with involuntary movement. Abruptly the mild twinge turned to sharp pricks traveling in waves like the earlier itches. He heard the slip-slip of small feet moving over the tiles, then there was a whispering in his ear. . . .

He was stretched out on ocher sand. Sand rippled out around him, empty, monotonous, to the circle of the horizon. Overhead the sky was blank, a deep dark blue, neither stars nor sun interrupting the satin sheen of the dome. He tried to move. He couldn't. His arms were pulled straight from his shoulders, his wrists tied to stakes with wide soft bands that felt like leather. He tugged experimentally at his right wrist. The strap clung to his wrist. He twisted and turned, wrenched at the stake but it was solid as a rooted watertree. His ankles were tied to stakes. He tried pulling with the stronger muscles of his legs. The pliant straps cut into his flesh and the stakes were set too solidly into the sand.

He looked down along his nude body. Between his feet he could see a lightening of the blue. An arc of orange bulged up past the flat curve of sand. Quickly the whole circle of the sun seemed to leap into the sky and he watched it climb rapidly toward zenith. He frowned. Too fast. It was climbing too fast. Getting hotter. Hotter. His flesh sucked in the heat. His eyes began to burn as the sun shone more and more directly into them. He closed his eyelids but the light burned through them, taking on a greenish tinge from the color of his skin. He felt sweat gathering on his skin. The drops grew, then began to run down into the crevices of his flesh. He burned. He burned. A dry tongue licked over already cracking lips. Too fast. Wrongness. He was drying out too fast. The inside of his mouth was leathery. Hard to swallow. Tongue felt rough, thick, a plug in his mouth. Hard to breathe. Thirsty. Meme Kalamah! Thirsty. The sun vibrated directly over him. Burning. Burning. It stopped moving. Stopped. Hot. So hot. Sweat sizzled on his burning skin. Water. . . .

The sky blinked. A great negation like the tolling of a monster bell cracked apart the scene. Then the sun was back. His lips moved. No. He croaked. The bell note came again and it was like the patter of rain on his frying skin. No. He joined his negation to the hidden bell and the sky shivered. No sun. The heat was broken and uneven. The light faltered. No sun. No. No desert. No. No thirst. No. No. No.

The heat and light vanished. The sky altered to white plasticrete ceiling. The gritty sand under his body smoothed to the heavy black cover on the laboratory table. Through the link that came back to his awareness when the desert vanished, he felt Aleytys's burst of relief and knew the great bell that helped him shatter the illusion was her negation flooding to him along the link. He felt a calm triumph. *We'll beat them*, he thought. *Star Hunter, together we'll beat these fools.* Then he was startled at himself, accepting a woman as partner. He began to realize how imperceptibly she'd been changing his ideas during their association. He touched her along the link, projecting ACCEPTANCE and felt her startled and appreciative response. He turned his head and watched the silent three at the panel. He laughed aloud, a lazy, teasing laugh that brought Haribu swinging around, his cold face showing a sudden irritation. Dallan backed away, nervous and shivering with fear.

There was an acrid stench floating about the room and a bluish haze drifting past Manoreh's face. Songoa fluttered about his console like a distressed mother hen, too fussed to bother about sounds from his experimental subject. Kell watched Manoreh for another minute then turned his back on him. "Can you go on?" His rich soft voice had grown harsh. Songoa sniffed resentfully. His thin lips were closed so tightly his mouth nearly disappeared as he glared at Haribu-Kell.

Manoreh watched, feeling apprehensive as he waited for the new attack.

Whispering down the link came Aleytys's soothing, cooling touch. It helped him endure the new series of itches passing over his head. When the itching turned to sharp nips, the soft susurration started in his ears again. He strained to make out the words. A clue . . . any clue. . . .

Kitosime bent over him, laughter in her dark eyes. He sat up, reached for her, and she danced away, her firm breasts bouncing under the roll knot of her dresscloth, her slim body elegant. She came close again, her hands teasing on him but when he tried to hold her, she slid away easily. She danced before him, avoiding his lunges. His blood heated. His hands glided over the silken skin. He couldn't hold her. She slid away from him with the same silent teasing laughter. He caught her and bore her down. Her face misted and changed. Blue coiling hair writhed out like red snakes. Aleytys. Her blue-green eyes were wide and mocking. She lay quietly beneath him and he felt a chill invading his body. "You'll be impotent with me, crawler in the mud." Her voice was low and mocking. Impotent. Nothing. He was limp and dead.

Nothing. He rolled over, turning his back on her to hide his shame.

A silver-green hand rubbed his arm. Long silver-green legs slid under his head. Kitosime held him on her lap, slim arms comforting him, touching him, gentle and tender, mother and lover. He was alive again, wanting her, wanting, breathing hard, erect, ready, a man again. He pulled her down against his face, took her nipple in his mouth.

He heard the chill, mocking laughter of the star woman. "Baby," she whispered. "Little boy." She pulled her breast free and slapped at him. "Rude baby. You a man? Hah!" His head cracked against the floor as she jerked her legs from under him and danced away.

In his agony he lay on the floor helpless, watching her flow back and forth, alternately gentle and cruel, Kitosime flowing into Aleytys, flowing, sensual, fire and passion, compassion, ambition, gentleness, driving need to win, silver-green arms, golden body, green flowing over gold over green, tight blue fleece springing into long silken strands of hair, whirling light upon the air as she danced, hard and soft, gold and green, red and indigo, one woman burning like fire into another cool and elegant, constantly altering, narrow elegance blooming into the taut but lush flesh of the Star Hunter. Constantly altering, mesmeric, enchanting, commanding. He curled in on himself. Shrinking. Shrinking. Smaller. Weaker. Retreating. Sinking to nothing. Die. I want to die. No more. Can't endure. No. No more. I . . . I . . . I . . . will . . . die . . . shrinking . . . shriveled . . . retreating . . . to the embryo . . . to nothing . . . I WILL . . . WILL . . . NOT . . . BE . . .

No! The negation thundered into his dimming senses. No, the bell tolled again. No. No. The great bell would not let him rest. Dark water flooded his shrinking, withered form, water cool and filled with life. No! The bell tolled and the water flowed faster over him. He straightened his body. The blended forms of Kitosime and Aleytys slid apart. Both came toward him. He shivered and drew back. No! the bell tolled. There was a pressure against his back. No more retreating. Kitosime touched him, her long slender fingers silver-green on green, warm, loving, supporting, mother and lover. Aleytys touched him. He stiffened. Her green-blue eyes were sad and soft. Her fingers ran along his arm, warm, gold, soft. The bell sang in his ears, drowning the ugly whispers, whispers he could not understand but whose evil intent was frustrated by the mellow tones of the bell. His body unfolded . . . unfolded . . . was hard and ready . . . a woman clinging to each arm . . . he pulled Aleytys against him . . . she flowed into him . . . gold flesh merging with green, the black water glowing, burning, expanding, driving outward . . . outward like a fireball expanding at the speed of light . . . destroying . . . burning . . . exploding. . . .

His mind returned to the lab. He was straining against the straps, the wave front of power still expanding. It seemed so slow, took years to move out, a glowing gold circle, it touched the console, seethed against it, brushed the metal with dandelion softness. Dallan, Songoa and Kell fell back, tumbling, blowing about, light as dandelion fluff. The console cracked apart, silent blue fire crawled, slow, slow, blue-white smoke crept out. Pieces of the machines sailed slow, slow, curving up, over, dropping light, skipping, skimming beside the splayed-out figures of Dallan, Songoa and Kell. And the anonymous white-coated attendants. And from somewhere outside came a great ear-numbing shriek of tormented metal and the hoarse scream of a man in torment that ceased with a dreadful suddenness.

Then everything moved faster; the pieces of the console slammed against the floor, flying debris slashing at the grunting, flailing forms of the men. The noise battered at him. Battered. His eyes rolled back. Blackness. Quiet. Nothing. . . .

Chapter XIV

★ ★ ★ ★ ★ ★ ★

Grey leaned against the bars, rubbed lightly the muscles of his arm though the itching was just below the shoulder muscles on his right side. The implant had made itself felt a little earlier. He closed his fingers into fists, then deliberately loosened them. *I want you loose to pry me out, she'd said.* He began prowling about the cage, muscles aching from his need to stay calm, in control. Control! He dropped beside the low door and stroked the cool metal. So easy, out of here in seconds. And then? He laughed suddenly, drawing a startled look from silent Faiseh sitting in the corner of the cage. Grey waved away the unspoken question and sat down, leaning against the bars. *In the trap now,* he thought. He closed his eyes and sought her. Twenty meters northwest, thirty meters up. Located in one of the cavities he'd plotted out before. Haribu's nest. He fidgeted, wondering if the time were now. Wondering if she wanted or needed his help. He looked up at an exclamation from Faiseh.

A figure was being carried on a stretcher from the gray-floored corridor. His bearers carted him into the lab. Grey raised his eyebrows. Faiseh nodded. "Manoreh," he said. He frowned. "Now?"

Grey looked down at his shaking hands. "No," he said suddenly. "Not yet." He smiled. "Let her move first."

Faiseh looked skeptical but went to watch the door into the lab.

Grey frowned. *Losing my center,* he thought. *Need to make the trek again.*

The trek. The winter trek into the Wildlands. A struggle to survive hunger, cold, fear, the endless dark solitude of the gray days and gray nights where night and day had no firm edges but merged with imperceptible slowness one into the other, where light was so diffuse most days that nothing had a shadow and all things took on the eerie unreality of nightmare. The trek. To make a great circle and lay his tokens on the cairns of Jothan and Linka and var-Himboldt. Add one more marked stone to the great stone piles at the three stages of the trek.

He could turn back with honor at the first, but forced himself on, taut with excitement and terror. He remembered looking into the gray haze over rock and snow, the endless cheating haze that tired the eyes and the spirit. He climbed carefully to the top of the cairn and added his stone to the others, then turned slowly. Without his Wolff-gift of direction he'd have lost himself a hundred times before he reached this spot. Circling cautiously on the unsteady top stones of the cairn, he saw nothing to mark the way ahead from the way he'd already crossed. Once again, he could turn back with honor. This time he hesitated. He was beaten fine by the ordeal, with little fat left on his bones. He stood on top of the cairn looking ahead into the haze but searching inside for the answer. The will . . . had he the will to go on?

When he made the third cairn he was a gaunt shadow in shadows. The mist had settled on the Wildlands, cold and chill, wrapping itself around him in clammy embrace. The sun was a pale ghost, a memory of a memory of warmth. A pack of silvercoats were close behind him, impossible to see, but he knew they were there, loping along his trail, bodies moving with clumsy grace over the snow. They were beautiful animals beautifully adapted to the winter. Two-layered coats, a dense white fluff hugging the long limber bodies and stiff silver-gray hairs lying sleekly atop the inner coat. Small round ears, a fluff of silver growing over mobile pink nostrils, double eyelids. Running on pads of fur, they moved in packs of four and five. Small animals, half a meter high at the shoulder, tireless and tenacious and disturbingly intelligent.

He climbed the cairn and placed his stone, then watched the silvercoats come out of the mist. He touched the darter at his belt, smiling grimly when he thought of his silent promise to himself that he'd return with magazine intact, supporting himself with knife and cord. *Thank god I didn't mouth that asininity*, he thought. He unsnapped the holster flap and touched the checking on the butt. The silvercoats faded into the mist. He was startled and misstepped, but caught himself before he fell. A twisted ankle here and his bones would roll about the plains in the summer winds.

High in pride, he leaped down the side of the cairn and went on into the fog. With taut excitement he looked around at the gray mist and the grey shadows of the silvercoats. He smiled with satisfaction, having at last decided on the name he'd take out of the Wildlands. "Grey," he murmured. His whisper fell dead into the cold, still air. And the silvercoats circled closer. His body ached with a fatigue that was harder to endure than the cold. But he smiled and moved steadily on.

The ground was beginning to rise. The snow was deeper, treacherously soft in spots, catching the tips of his snowshoes. He moved slowly, senses alert as he'd never been alert before—as if his nerve ends stretched beyond his skin and tasted the air, the fog, the snow. He saw everything. At the same time, he was intensely aware that he had in Wolff a deadly opponent, an enemy who would kill him at the first slip he made.

When the faint sun glow dipped toward the horizon he stopped and built a shelter, cutting the snow with his snow knife and laying the blocks in an ascending spiral. After settling the key block in the center hole, he cut an entrance and rolled out, coming to his feet with a spring that disconcerted two silvercoats creeping nearer. He blocked the entrance and went out to hunt fuel and food.

He spent nine days there, eating greedily the fat of his kills for the energy he needed to fight off the debilitating effects of the cold. Nine days. Long, endless days, when after the excitement of the hunt, there was nothing to do but think. On the trail his body moved and was, and that was sufficient. His legs moved in a rhythm that blanked the mind until he saw and was not conscious that he saw, heard and was not conscious that he heard. Time flowed past him, serene and unnoticed, until the end of the day came to him with a degree of surprise. And on the hunt, he was focused on the prey, intensely aware of the moment, aware also, as an animal would not be, of the future, able to plan, both more and less than animal.

Now his body was quiet, retracted into itself. His mind awakened and brought black depression at first, a loneliness and a consciousness that he was a fool, a stiff-necked fool driven by pride to surpass his ancestors. To raise a new cairn,

Grey's cairn, a marker to his megalomania, to force an acknowledgment from history of his existence. To raise a monument to his endurance and skill, when he knew he was a fool and that a pile of rocks would be a monument to his stupidity in letting his pride and his need for something that he couldn't explain even to himself drive him far beyond what he could reasonably ask of body, mind and luck. And he knew, despite his recognition of his stupidity, he would go on a full cairn-length and roll the stones together to mark his passage.

He sat in the quiet, chill darkness of his shelter and listened to the ice melt drip endlessly from the snow blocks, reliving a dozen times each humiliation he'd suffered in his score of years, until finally he moved beyond these into dreams of the future that grew wilder and wilder until he was hallucinating—moved beyond that into the simple contemplation of the contents of the shelter, seeing them in the uncertain flicker of the crude oil lamp with an abrupt new clarity and wonder.

On the ninth day he left the shelter, saluting the skulking silvercoats with a grave appreciation of their beauty and worth.

At the foot of a thirty-meter cliff swept clean by icy winds, he built his cairn and carved his name into the cliffside. He stepped back, examined the crude letters and thought he should add something to tell the passerby what he'd learned in the silence of the shelter. Then he shook his head. *Grey*. It was enough. Whoever came here would have found his own peace. In any case there were no words for what he wanted to say.

On the third day of his back-trek he was forced to kill two of the silvercoats. They came at him without warning as he rolled out of the snow shelter into the dim light of morning, came silent and vicious, hitting him from both sides. But they misjudged the speed of his cautionary roll and he was on his feet beyond them, darter in hand, before they could scramble around. He put darts into the snarling faces, feeling a deep regret when the dead predators crashed against his legs. The other silvercoats were hidden in the mist. He left the bodies lying in the darkening crimson of their blood and went on.

One by one the other silvercoats came at him, forcing him to kill them. But he was settled into the deep calm he fought for alone that nine days in the shelter. And he survived. . . .

In the cage he sat struggling to recapture some of that detachment earned fifteen standard years before. Fifteen years. *I need to make the trek again.* He repeated to himself. *With Aleytys this time, if she'll come. I've forgotten too much.*

"What about her? She was with him," Faiseh said suddenly.

"She's here," Grey told him. "Wait a bit more."

The lift beside the hareblock opened and the Vryhh stepped out. He walked briskly to the lab and moved inside. Grey rose to his knees, hesitated, looked at Faiseh, brooding over the bit of lab he could see through the arch. Grey bent over the lock and began using the force fields in his fingers to coax it open.

Behind him the metal egg began to thrum. The sound shrilled higher and higher until the egg was shrieking. Then it sat silent and unmoved for a few minutes. After this pause it began humming again. The hum rose and fell, stopped altogether, then came again, louder and louder, shriller and shriller, until the egg shook on its base. The watuk controller clawed at his head trying to jerk the cap off but his hands shook so uncontrollably he couldn't get a grip on it.

Then the egg exploded, hurling shards of metal in all directions. Grey dropped onto his face. The watuk shrieked, then slumped over, as scores of the metal pieces sliced through him. Blood gushed from his twitching body then slowed and stopped as he died. Pieces of the egg slammed against the cage and ricocheted with a high, whining noise.

Grey was on his knees again before the metal stopped flying. He knelt by the lock and had it open when he heard Faiseh suck in his breath. He looked around. The Vryhh was running from the lab. He stopped by the shattered egg, flinging out his arms with a howl of rage that filled the cavern. "Bitch!" he screamed. "Bitch. . . ." Muttering wildly he ran into the lift and sent it upward.

Kitosime smiled down at the boys sitting in a half circle around the powerstones. The small shrine was hot and stifling now that the rain had stopped, The boys shifted uneasily, their slit pupils almost round in the dim light. She bent over them and touched each upturned face, then moved back to stand in the open doorway. "You should be safe here. I'll lock the door." She held up the large key. "Fa-men won't disturb a shrine. They may try the door. But you all keep very quiet and they'll go away again." She touched the eyestones in the pouch around her neck. "I know it's not an easy place to be. But you are welcome here, I promise you." She smiled at each in turn. "You all right?"

The boys nodded. But she could feel their discomfort as she shut the door on them and locked it. She looked up. A few drops fell on her face, but the clouds were shredded and the sun was hotter than before, leaching steam from the thatched roof of the shrine.

She walked slowly down the manstairs and stopped outside the dormitory. She pushed the door open. Mara and S'kiliza were finishing the last bed. Hodarzu sat playing with his blocks, content to be with the girls. Kitosime nodded at them. "Good," she said. "You got up all the blood on the porch?"

Mara nodded. A small smile turned up the corners of her full mouth. "Wash whole porch with lye. No hound pick up scent there."

Kitosime laughed, but shook her head. "If you want to join the boys. . . ."

Mara shook her head vigorously. There was a bright glitter in her indigo eyes. "Make fool of them, the. . . ." She couldn't find the word she wanted in her limited new vocabulary, but she projected a fierce hatred.

"S'kiliza?"

The younger girl grinned at her, came over, and took Mara's hand.

"Well, then. . . ." Kitosime sighed. "You know your roles. Mara, you're Bighouse girl and S'kiliza's your bound-girl attendant. She also takes care of Hodarzu. You know the discipline, both of you. Think carefully, my little ones. Can you hold in front of Fa-men?"

Once again they both nodded. Kitosime moved back to the door. "Mara, come to my room when you're finished here. We need to put the last polish on you. S'kiliza, take Hodarzu down to the water garden." She studied the small, neat form in the plain dresscloth. "You look fine as you are, Siki. Don't let Hodarzu get you too mussed."

In her own room on the floor below, she changed into her most striking dresscloth, a pattern of waterdrops in alternating white and black falling across wide diagonals of solid white and black. She had no one to help her dress her hair in its coils of small braids so she drew it into a tight spiraling knot on top of her head and twisted a gold chain about the spiral. She chose earrings to match, gold hoops that swung gently beside her neck. When Mara came in, she was buffing her nails. "Sit on the bed, little one," she said. "Give me your hands."

She took Mara's small hand. "Could be worse. You kept them washed, didn't you?"

Mara nodded. "Bad feeling being dirty. I hate it. But if I try to get in house. . . ." She shivered.

Kitosime began buffing the short, square nails. "It comes back fast now, doesn't it." She finished with one hand and took the other. "I'll put on some henna when I've done your feet. Remember, Mara. Every move is studied, graceful. You are submissive in the presence of men, bending like a willow wand. Say nothing without thinking first. Do nothing without thinking first. Don't let them startle you into something unconsidered." She set the small foot down then reached for the henna cream.

"I know, 'Tosime. As you say, it come back fast."

The Fa-men came clattering through the arch, the hounds snarling before them. Four men clad in fine-dressed chul fur with blood-stained assegais slung across their backs, their burnished tips gleaming in Jua Churukuu's strengthening light. Their hair was braided as elaborately as a woman's, a silver ring hung from the left ear of each, arm rings of silver clasped around upper arms. And scars, four of them, slashed across the right cheek. They were images out of an almost forgotten past, creatures of the mythic time before the Families united and drove Watulkingu from its tribal anarchy.

Kitosime stood on the porch, a silent, elegant figure, her serenity forcing them to control their eagerness and adopt proper manners. The hounds ran at her. She didn't move, stood quietly waiting for the Fa-kichwa to call them off.

He heeled the faras forward, driving it between Kitosime and the hounds. With a doubled leather strap he beat them back and drove them out of the court. Then he rode to the foot of the stairs. He looked across at her, his eyes bold and appreciative. "I've seen you, lady. You're Kitosime the favored."

She inclined her head but said nothing.

"Where is Old Man Kobe?" He scanned the court, then the face of the building. "Or are you here alone?"

She moved a hand in graceful negation. "My son stays with me, and a girlchild in my care with her bondservant. I know nothing of Old Man Kobe or the others. She in my care and I went with my son to Legba's shrine on pilgrimage. When we returned from the mountains, the Holding was as you see. The bondman serving us went to search for them and has not returned. We have been here since." She spread out her hands, letting him see their lovely shape, the faint red stain of the henna.

"The hares walk, lady."

Her hands fluttered in delicate helplessness. "Where would we go? We have been quiet and undisturbed here."

He backed his faras up and reined it in to face Sniffer and Fireman and Second, then led it around until it stepped daintily in front of her again. "We trailed a wilding male here."

"Here?" Her doll mask firmly in place, she fluttered her eyelashes at him. "Kobe's will is known. They wouldn't dare."

He scowled at her, suspecting something was wrong. Some nuance in her behavior or voice it might be, or nothing at all. "Your son is here?"

"My charge and her bondservant have him in the water garden." She stared past him out of the arch. "A wilding male?" She shivered delicately. "You tracked him here?"

The Fa-kichwa scowled in annoyance. "The rain washed away his trail, but he was close to this Holding." He slid off his mount, motioning the others to follow his lead. "We're tired and wet, lady. A mug of cha would comfort us. As you say, Kobe's will is known in these things."

Kitosime bowed her head, holding desperately to her doll mask, silently blessing the hard training Kobe had unknowingly given her. She led them to the kitchen and put water on to boil. *Meme Kalamah, give me strength.* She touched the eyestones in the neck pouch and felt them move warmly under her fingers. Comforted a little, she set four mugs on the table in front of men whose eyes watched her avidly.

She wanted to stand silent and let them wait until the water boiled, but that would be a flagrant breach of training, so she bowed her head over her hands. "Is there anything else I can find for you, eM'zeesh?"

"Food would be welcome, lady."

She made an apologetic gesture. "I know little of cooking, eM'zeesh. But there is cheese and meat and bread."

"Bring it, lady."

She bowed again and left them, going to the cold cellar to fetch the food. With smoked kudu and cheese in a basket, she sank onto the bottom step of the stairs and stared into the chill darkness of the cellar. She didn't want to go back into that kitchen. "Meme Kalamah," she whispered. "I'm afraid. His eyes, the way he looks at me . . . the way they all look at me. . . . He's still afraid to touch me, afraid of Kobe. But Kobe isn't here. How long will that fear last?" She bent over the basket, her hand closed over the pouch with the eyestones, a cold nausea twisting her stomach. "I can't bear it if he forces me. . . ."

After another minute, she wiped a hand over her sweating face. The children were depending on her. She touched the eyestones once more and climbed slowly up the stairs. The hand that pushed open the door was shaking. She paused a moment to discipline her body, then she glided into the kitchen and placed the food on the table in front of the men. She brought knives then stepped back. She was Bighouse. It wasn't her role to serve food. Backing away gracefully, she crossed to the outwall and stood close to the rough stone, like an elegant, blank-faced statue. *Carved by Kobe*, she thought. *Polished by time. Endless, unendurable time.*

The Fa-men ate in silence for several minutes, then the kichwa banged his mug down on the polished wood of the table. "You said your son is here, lady?"

"In the water garden with the boundgirl and she who is in my care." She kept her voice low and musical, letting none of her tension show. There was a cold sickness in her stomach. She fought to control it as she waited for the man to go on.

"His father is suspect. Wild Ranger, running around out beyond the Jinolimas instead of following custom and working his father's land. Rumors say your son might be tainted also." His fingers had tightened around the mug as if he were strangling something.

When she could trust her voice, she said quietly, "I am Kitosime the favored. So people lie."

He nodded. "True, lady. Best the boy be tested."

Kitosime's knees began to shake. Her hand closed over the eyestones. The feel of the talisman gave her strength. She raised her eyes. "The Old Man has plans for Hodarzu. He would not like being crossed."

"Be at ease, lady. The testing won't hurt the boy. If he's free of taint, all the better to have it proved and mark the rumors for the lies they are." His lips stretched into a travesty of a smile as his eyes followed the line of her body.

If he touches me, she thought, *he'll have to kill me to keep Kobe from finding out. And the children . . . ah the children. . . . He's getting closer to it. Only his fear of Fa and Kobe holds him back now.* "I'll get him," she said.

"No!" His eyes narrowed. He looked slowly from face to face. Second. Sniffer. Fireman. The Second was a chunky man with wild eyes. The paired scars on his cheek twitched continually. Fa-kichwa nodded at him. "Get the boy."

Second rose and stumped out of the room. He seldom spoke and said nothing this time.

Fa-kichwa turned back to Kitosime. "Kobe's blood is good," he said slowly, his eyes glowing with fanaticism. "But, by Fa's breath, if your son is tarred with wild, Fa's claim comes above all others. Old Man Kobe knows that well enough." His eyes narrowed. His thin lips stretched into a significant smile. "You are young, lady. There will be other children. You might find a father for them with untainted blood."

She kept her face still with an effort. "For my honor, Fa-kichwa, I may not understand you. For my father's honor."

The door swung open and Mara came quietly into the kitchen. She held her head high and walked with careful grace. S'kiliza followed, Hodarzu's hand clutched tightly in hers. They crossed to Kitosime who came a few steps away from the wall to meet them. She was proud of them and knew that she felt that pride, that it strengthened her. S'kiliza came to her right and Mara to her left. She put a hand on each girl's shoulder and faced the Fa-kichwa. "This is not necessary."

"Fa requires," he mumbled. His eyes no longer caressed her. They were fixed on the boy, shining with a different kind of lust. *He wants Hodarzu to fail*, she thought. *He wants to see him writhing in the fire.*

She reached down and lifted her son into her arms. "The girls should not have to watch this," she said firmly.

Fa-kichwa shrugged indifferently. "Let them go, then."

Kitosime looked first at Mara then at S'kiliza. She felt their resistance and shook her head. "You must," she said quietly. "Wait for us in the water garden." She pushed Mara gently toward the door. "Siki, please." She swung around and touched the smaller girl's cheek. "Go."

Holding Hodarzu against her breast, she watched them leave, then turned to the Fa-kichwa. "This isn't necessary," she repeated.

He ignored her words and held out his arms. "The boy."

Kitosime backed away from him until she was pressed against the wall. "What are you going to do? I won't let you hurt him." Hodarzu started crying, his first whimpers turning to full-throated howls as he responded to her terror and her anger. She tried to soothe him but couldn't soothe herself and that was the problem. His small body was warm and heavy in her straining arms. Abruptly she was angry at Kobe and Manoreh and every male ancestor for what they had done to her, were doing to her now, for keeping her ignorant and for despising her so thoroughly that her feelings and needs meant less than nothing to them—who not only tolerated but actively supported this abomination of bigotry and hatred, this blood and death in the name of morality, this denial of the gift of life.

Fa-kichwa snorted impatiently and pulled Hodarzu from her arms. The Second and the Fireman held her back as he took the boy to the center of the kitchen. Gasping, angry now almost to the point of the male blindrage, she fought against them, kicking, stretching her neck, to bite hands, arms, any flesh within range. All she achieved was the loosening of the rollknot of her dresscloth. She felt the cloth begin to slip and stopped struggling abruptly. To bare her body before these animals—the thought sent chills into her soul.

She straightened and stood still. Then she turned her head slowly to the Second. "Let me loose," she said quietly, Kobe's daughter again.

"Keep your place, lady," he muttered, but he took his hands off her arm.

She glanced at the Fireman and he stepped aside, releasing her. She tightened the rollknot and stabbed her broochpin through the folds. She deftly tucked back the hair pulled loose in her struggle. *Fool*, she thought, *all I have is Kobe's name to fight these carrion birds. No, double fool, I have this.* She closed her hand around the pouch with the eyestones and felt a stirring.

During her brief struggle, Fa-kichwa had walked away carrying the small howling boy. Hodarzu's face squeezed into a mask of wrinkles; tears oozed from his tight shut eyes. Fakichwa ignored that and sat him down hard on the cold tiles. The boy tried to scramble to his feet and run to his mother, but the man slapped him hard across the face and pushed him back down.

Kitosime's face burned. Her hand tightened around the stones. She whispered to her son, "Be quiet, my baby, be quiet." At the same time she projected CALM/TRUST/QUIET.

Hodarzu stopped crying abruptly and stared up at the man crouched over him. Bewildered, he looked around for his mother, not understanding what was happening. He'd never been struck before. He flinched as the Fa-kichwa's hand rose again, but the waves of CALM flowing from his mother comforted him, held him quiet.

"Sit there, boy," Fa-kichwa said sternly. "Sniffer."

The twisted little man scuttled over to him.

"You'll need Muwura."

"Was some in water garden. Second found it, brought it." Second thrust a rather withered branch from a small woody plant into his wrinkled claw.

Sniffer took it and sniffed at it. "Late in the year for a testing, but the muwura's still potent." He held it up. Wing-shaped gray-green leaves marched along a brown stem in matched pairs. He ran his thumb along the leaves. They quivered and curled up. Sniffer nodded, jerking his ugly head. "Potent enough," he repeated.

Kitosime took a step forward and stopped as the Fireman grabbed her arm. When she stared at him, he dropped his hand, but shook his head warningly. "Don't interfere, lady."

Kitosime was fighting a growing numbness born of terror and helplessness.

A warmth invaded her hand. The small lumps bruising her palm stirred. She stepped back until she was pressed against stone, the wall giving strength to her shaking body. She loosed her agonized grip a little as a new warmth spread up her arm and filled her with power. The air in the kitchen turned a rich gold before her eyes, shimmering like firelit water. The figures of the Fa-men dissolved into the golden haze, became black, oily quavers. The stones clicked against her palm in a quickening rhythm.

Her sight cleared. Hodarzu was staring up at the Fa-kichwa, his eyes huge and solemn in his small round face. He wasn't frightened any more. Kitosime could feel the power reaching out from her, calming him, folding him within its tender glow.

Fa-kichwa slapped him across the face again, shouted at him, leaned over until his scarred face almost touched the boy and made ugly animal noises at him.

Sniffer knelt beside Fa-kichwa. When Fa-kichwa sank back on his heels, Sniffer took over, shouting at Hodarzu, slapping him, squealing in his face. Hodarzu was puzzled by all this and a little frightened. But the feel of his mother surrounding him with warmth and comfort steadied him. He began to find the men funny. He started giggling at their antics.

Sniffer scowled and thrust the muwura into the boy's face.

Hodarzu giggled again. The golden glow enfolded him, kept him warm and safe.

The air shivered and shivered around Kitosime. The stones burned into her hand. She could feel her flesh charring. The pain filled her. She trembled. What was happening—what. . . .

Sniffer howled and thrust the muwura at Hodarzu again.

The stones clicked, burned. Kitosime sagged against the stone.

The frond was still, trembling only with the shaking of Sniffer's hand. The wing-shaped leaves spread out over the boy's laughing face.

Sniffer growled, sour with disappointment. He thrust the muwura again at the boy. Hodarzu reached for the leaves. Sniffer snatched them away and crushed the muwura in his hand. "The boy is clean," he muttered.

The stones went dead. Kitosime's stiff fingers uncramped from around the pouch. She let her hand fall. For the first time she became aware of the coldness and roughness of the stone against her back and of the ache of her slowly relaxing muscles.

Fa-kichwa looked uneasy. Hodarzu was Kobe's grandson. What plans Kobe had for him. . . . . His eyes flicked to Kitosime then back to the boy.

Kitosime straightened. This was a dangerous moment. Fa-kichwa was afraid and his fear made him unpredictable. She walked carefully to the center of the room and picked up Hodarzu. The boy clung to her, growing a little frightened now that the warmth was gone from around him. Suppressing the anger that flared from the ashes of her terror, she turned her back on the silent Fa-men and moved to the door, her body falling automatically into the Bighouse walk.

In the doorway she turned, "This house is yours, Fa-men. By Kobe's will, I must have it so. For my honor I must ask that you leave me in peace with the children." She gently stroked Hodarzu's back. "You will confirm to Old Man that his grandson tested free of taint?"

Fa-kichwa looked relieved. "I will confirm." His voice was harsh, stern as he regained his fanatic's certainty of his righteousness.

She walked out and left him looking around. Before the door closed behind her, he was pouring a cup of cha for himself.

Kitosime walked swiftly toward the stairs. His breath hot on her shoulder, Hodarzu murmured, "Bad mans. Silly mans." Then he stirred in her arms, disturbed by her anger and fear.

She began climbing the stairs, humming softly, rubbing her hand along his back, soothing him into drowsiness. As she elbowed the dormitory door open, she murmured, "A nice nap, Toto. Maybe when you wake, the bad men will be gone. Gone." She laid him on his bed and pulled the cover over him. She knelt on the floor beside him, humming again, projecting SLEEPINESS/CALM/TENDERNESS. She touched his small face gently, smoothed her hands over his small form until he fell deep asleep.

She drew her knees up and leaned against the wall, sitting between two narrow beds in the rows of narrow beds. She examined her hands. Shaking. So tired. She lifted high her left hand that still burned where the eyestones had touched it. She brought it close to her face, examined it. The flesh was unmarked. "I am the vessel," she murmured. "Through me earth speaks, sky speaks." It was a terrifying thing to think, let alone express in words, but she was too tired to accept that terror within herself. Too many fears had worn out her mind and body. She closed her eyes and drowsed a little while beside her sleeping son.

But her rest was disturbed by nightmare. Reluctantly she opened aching eyes. *The girls . . . They should be waiting in the garden . . . I don't trust those beasts . . . I should go down now . . . and the boys in the shrine . . . when will those beasts leave? When will they leave . . . and will they*

*come back. . . How many times will they come back . . .
How much longer until I can't hold them off . . . We have to
leave this place . . . soon . . . but where to go . . . Where
can we go that they won't follow? And how can we get
away?*

Her thoughts began to circle again into nightmare. She
jerked herself upright and rubbed at her eyes. *The girls, got
to go down.*

She struggled to her feet and stood swaying with weariness.
Hodarzu slept deeply. She bent over him briefly, touched his
soft cheek. She caught a glimpse of herself mirrored in window glass. There was an anguish in the twisted features that
troubled her. Her mask was dissolved. She smoothed her
hand across her face. Eyes on the ghost image in the glass,
she arranged her features into the emptiness of her elegant
mask. Then she glided noiselessly out the door, stopping
briefly to take a last look at her son, and went down the
stairs. When she passed the kitchen, she heard the voices.
"Go home, beasts," she whispered, but she turned aside and
almost ran through the house to the water garden,

Aleytys felt the power ripped out of her; like a tiderace it
tore down the link, passing through Manoreh and out again
until she felt the out-puff of the explosion, saw through Manoreh's eyes the flaring out of the goldcircle, the slow-motion
destruction of the lab, heard through his ears the final crash-
ing of the controller and the screams of the wounded. Then
the vision slammed to blackness. Manoreh was unconscious.
Not dead, she thought, *I feel him alive, I feel his heart beat.*
Then she leaped from the bed and danced around the room
as a wild exuberance consumed her. "We did it! We did it!"
She laughed and whirled about then threw herself back on
the bed, bouncing and giggling.

The door whooshed open and Kell was standing there, his
face contorted with rage. He crossed the room in great leaps,
bounding grotesquely. He pulled her to her feet. His fist
slammed into her ribs. Pain exploded through her. He began
to beat her face and breasts, stomach and legs. At first she
resisted, lifting her hands to fend him off, struggled, tried to
break away. Then there was only pain, nothing but pain. Her
strength was nothing against his metal skeleton. She was
locked in her head, locked away from the talents. *Harskari,
help me*, she cried out into the darkness. *Help me.* When no

answer reached her, she tried to let go of consciousness. Her tough Vryhh-bred body defeated her. Pain, endless pain. No subtle torture this, just endless brute pain . . . bones broke . . . she was bleeding inside . . . face a ruin . . . bones shattered . . . splintered shoulder . . . rib stabbing through a lung . . . bleeding, torn inside . . . and her body would not loose its stubborn hold on life and consciousness.

Breathing hard, Kell dropped her onto the bed. She could not see, eyes flooded with sticky blood. She could hear him moving, hear the breath hissing through his teeth. A warm liquid splashed over her, stinging the cuts, a familiar acrid smell. He was urinating on her. She retched; in spite of the pain, she spat out sour fluid from her stomach. Moaned. Moved her head feebly.

She heard a short, sharp yelp. Another. Low-voiced cursing in a language she didn't know—the whisper of feet moving away across the rug. Then the claustrophobic tightening around her head was gone. "Heal yourself, mud." His voice was taut with pain. She wondered vaguely about that, then began weaving a forceweb around her shattered body. Before she tightened it she tapped the black water, used the power to block off the pain, then pulled the web taut and let the water flow to heal. The web worked, shaped, remolded the shards of bone and the torn and bruised body. Inside and out, the web and the water restored her physical integrity. And the pain of the healing was greater than the wounding—pain was fire burning her, an agony so intense she died a thousand times because she could not possibly endure it, but she did endure it. The moment the healing was finished, she wove another web about the inhibitor coiled like a viper around her spine and flung it through the still open door.

After the vibration of the small explosion died, she heard Kell laugh shrilly. "So be it, mud," he said. His voice was harsh. "Come here."

She sat up slowly and rubbed her eyes open. He was in the pneumochair, his broken hands cradled in his lap. She looked at them and understood. In his fury he'd forgotten his fragility and been careless with his blows.

"Come here," he said. "Heal these." He lifted his hands, then let them drop.

She slid off the bed, her eyes fixed on his. In spite of all the horror he woke in her, she was drawn irresistibly toward him. More than in anything else, she found her reality in her healing gift. It was the one thing that had never wholly betrayed her. The need to use the gift was like a craving for drugs. She touched the Vryhh's hands carefully, unconcerned for his evil and the harm he intended her. The need drove her. She reached for her water and let it flow into him until the withered flesh was whole again and the chalky bones mended.

Before he could move, she was on her feet and away. She glanced briefly at the door then ignored it. The battle was joined between them now and wouldn't end until one was defeated. She retreated until her back was against the wall, then faced him, excitement glittering through her. She was breathing rapidly, her heart slammed in her throat. She gathered herself and hurled a force hammer at him.

Off balance, he barely deflected her thrust. He settled back in the chair and tossed a blanketing blackness over her.

It smothered her, tightening, strangling. She slashed at it with rage knives and pain knives, shredded it, threw shimmering silver rage knives at him.

All deflected. Countered by a stinking ooze of envy, hatred, malice that sickened her and sapped her will to resist. He bent forward, using physical presence to heighten the pressure on her. She fumbled. His greenstone eyes glittered. She burned. Clean red and blue flames caught at the ooze, smoldered, struggled, then flared it to ash. Clean ash. She gathered the flames and threw them at him.

Deflected. He seemed to grow stronger as if he drank her strength. He gathered in the shattered flames that drifted around him, sucked them one by one into his body. He seemed to expand. A giant. Towering over her. Pressing down on her. Flame hair writhing about his white face. Green eyes cold, filled with a cold, cold hatred. Cold slowed her, emptied her of rage, of the will to fight.

Cold . . . she shivered . . . terror . . . helplessness . . . he was too strong . . . knew too much . . . too old. She dropped to her knees, crouched shivering . . . ice layered over her, began pressing down on her, enclosing her.

The diadem chimed. The room filled with its glow. Shadith's purple eyes snapped open. "Lee, fool, you're striking at his strength. The exoskeleton. Hit his power source. Pin him to that chair with the weight of the metal!"

Amber eyes opened. Harskari said briskly, "Strike, daughter. We will defend."

Black eyes. Swardheld. "Get him, freyka." He grinned and lifted his great two-handed sword. Symbolic only, still it gave her a sense of strength she could lean against and fueled her confidence in herself.

Kell sneered and pressed harder, still supremely confident of a quick and thorough victory. His brilliant green eyes grew larger as he beat at her, slamming his force against her, tap-tap-tap, easy at first then harder and harder until her head jerked in rhythm with it.

Leaving her defense to the Three, she slipped beneath the bludgeoning and tickled at the Vryhh's exoskeleton hunting a weakness, searching for the power points. So intent was he on crushing her he didn't feel her fingers closing around the cells that drove the metal skeleton. With a cry of triumph, she wrenched them loose and threw them across the room. They fell with a tiny pattering like a fistful of rice cast against stone.

He was off balance. The sudden lifeless weight of the metal dragged him back, plastered him against the chair. His hands were pinned to his meager thighs. His head was jerked back until he glared at the ceiling.

The pressure on Aleytys vanished. She heard his breathing grow harsh and ragged as his skeleton-supported lungs began to fail. Rubbing at her forehead she struggled to her feet and staggered to the bed. She dropped onto the end and rubbed the heels of her hands across her aching eyes. "Harskari?" They were gone. Loneliness was raw and new again as if the days she'd spent learning to accept her loss had never been. Alone. Without kin or kind. *How can I live?* she thought. She looked at the Vryhh. *Monster . . . and kin? Is that what Vrya are like? My mother. . . .* An intense longing to know her mother swept over her.

The rasp of Kell's breathing drew her attention. His face was turning blue. She slid off the bed and walked over to him. His eyes were open. When she bent over him, they fixed on her with a cold determination that caused her to shiver. Avoiding that malignant stare, she began examining his clothing, twitching the heavy cloth about, looking for openings. He tried to fight her, but his strength failed and his breathing grew more labored. In seconds he was forced to let her do as she pleased with him.

She worked the clothing from his body. It shocked her and woke a pity in her she knew he would hate. His skin was dry, large pieces of it sloughing off to uncover livid bruises, great sickening patches of green, purple and ocher. He was a barely fleshed skeleton in a cage of gray metal. She watched his decaying chest rise and fall slightly, hampered by the weight of the metal. The exoskeleton was a beautifully crafted instrument that sheltered him and kept him mobile. Now it was killing him. She fumbled at it, but there was no way she could find to take it off. Parts of it seemed to be sealed to the bone and there were elaborate neural connections.

She bent over him, staring down into that baleful green gaze. *Kin to me,* she thought, amused at the absurdity of her sentimentality. *My luck. First relative I meet is this thing.* She touched the great artery pulsing in his throat. *Press on this, be a mercy almost. He threatens me. He threatens my son.*

She pulled her hand away, flexing the fingers. He disgusted her. But her fingers itched with the need to heal. He was sick. *He deserves to die if anyone ever did,* she thought. *He ought to die. I wonder if I could . . . Serd-Amachar. No cure.* She pressed her hand to his taut midsection, on the rotten flesh the skeleton left bare.

It was the hardest, most exhausting, most painful experience she'd ever called down on herself; the agony stretched on forever in a battle longer and harder than her struggle with Kell. The disease was tenacious, clinging to the wasted cells, but at last the black water flushed the sickness away and sparked the rebuilding of the flesh.

Aleytys broke contact before this had gone on long. The exoskeleton fit too closely. Kell would have to have it removed as his tissues plumped out. She sighed. Once again her resources were depleted. She reached back to the river. It was so thin and mistlike that her healing was slow and uncertain. She let herself down until she was sitting beside the pneumochair. She'd called on it more during the past minutes. *Minutes?* She rubbed at her aching back. *Minutes. The whole battle. Five minutes? Certainly not more than ten. My god,* she thought.

She heard the pounding of feet and jumped up, backing away from the naked Vryhh, then relaxing as Grey plunged through the door.

He stopped when he saw her. "You all right?" He moved to stand over the Vryhh. "Playing games?"

Aleytys walked to the bed and scooped up the dress from the floor beside it. "Dirty mind, shame-shame, Grey." She giggled. "Look at him. You think I would?" She slipped the green velvet over her head, kicking away the jewels, then smoothed her hands down over the velvet to settle the dress in place. She crossed to Grey. "What's happening out there?"

Grey jerked a thumb at the Vryhh. "What about him?"

She grinned. "Don't worry. I've defused him; he's pinned in that chair by the weight of the metal."

Kell turned his head slowly and focused on her. "Run, half-ling," he whispered. "Twist and turn, struggle as you will, animal, you're mine. I know you now. I know you."

She shivered and pulled Grey toward the door. "We can pick him up later. Where are Manoreh and Faiseh?"

Chapter XV

★ ★ ★ ★ ★ ★ ★

Kitosime sat against the railing of the roof walk. The four boys knelt beside her where they could reach out and touch her, draining off some of their nervous excitement. The long spell in the shrine had worn them now. It wasn't an easy place to stay, especially at night.

Liado pressed his face to the uprights of the fence, staring out over the plain. The Fa-men had stayed the night, forcing the boys to remain in hiding. Kitosime had slipped them some food and a pot of cha in the middle of the night and stayed a little while to comfort them. She'd sat in the uneasy darkness, hugging and stroking them until they'd calmed enough to sleep. All but Liado. He'd tried. She had to leave him curled up in a miserable lump against the wall as if the solidity of the wood gave him some assurance.

When she'd let them out after the Fa-men had ridden off, he'd flown out of the darkness, his small body nearly knocking her off her feet. He clutched at her, shaking so hard he couldn't stand. He made no sound, just held on. Now he clung to the uprights, still shivering occasionally.

Fa-kichwa Gakpeh had stopped her in the kitchen, grabbing her arm. "We hunt the wildings today. Don't worry, lady. We will be back at nightfall to protect you."

Kitosime stood very still. She inclined her head, heavy eyelids falling over eyes that might have betrayed her horror.

With reluctance he let go her arm, then he wheeled and marched out with an absurd pomposity that should have been ridiculous but was not.

Now Liado was watching for them, his small body knotted with tension.

Cheo scratched at the side of his hand. "Kichwa bother you," he said suddenly.

Kitosime looked at him, startled. "How. . . ."

140

"When you speak of him. . . ." Cheo sought words then shrugged and projected DISGUST/HORROR/FEAR. He touched Amea's thigh and the bigger boy nodded.

"We help?" Amea said slowly. Words were very difficult for him still. He understood more and more but spoke little.

"No," she said firmly. "You help me most when I don't have to worry about you."

Cheo frowned. "I think we kill him quick before he hurt you." Amea growled, an angry sound deep in his throat.

Kitosime reached out a hand to each. "No, no, my little ones, no, Toto-angi. Not until we have to. I know. I know. Yes he threatens me, us, all of us. But he's too dangerous. They all are. Promise me you'll tell me before you do anything. Promise me!" She bent forward earnestly. "Promise me!"

Before they could answer, Liado whimpered, patting at her shoulder to get her attention. She swung around. Cheo, Amea, and Wame scooted forward until they could see also.

The Fa-men were riding down the red dirt road outside the emwilea hedge, heading back for the house. They rode slowly because of the string of wilding children that trotted among them, a rope looped about their necks, tying them from the Fa-kichwa's faras to the Fireman's mount. Second and Sniffer rode beside them, looking down repeatedly at their catch.

Kitosime could read their satisfaction even at that distance. "Meme Kalamah," she whispered. "A burning."

The boys pressed against her. She closed one hand about the eyestones and closed the other about the railing, trying to fight off the stifling outflow of terror and rage. "Help me," she said softly. Amea gulped. He closed his eyes and struggled back from the edge of blindrage, carrying Wame and Cheo with him into a measure of calm. Kitosime flashed PRIDE at him and turned back to watching the Fa-men coming closer and closer. Cheo leaned past her shoulder. "We let them loose," he whispered into her ear.

Kitosime nodded. "Tonight," she said quietly. "They light the Fa-fire at dawn and keep watch by turns during the night, except for Fireman who lays the fire and dedicates it to Fa. At least, that's what I've picked up, listening to Kobe talk." She closed her eyes and swallowed her sudden flare of old anger. *Forgotten. Kneeling blank-faced beside the Old Man as he chatted with furred and scarred visitors. Hearing . . . hearing. . . .* She rose unsteadily to her feet. "I've got to get downstairs before they come in. Amea, take care of the others. Here." She handed him the key. "You can lock the door from inside. Please do lock it. They could come up here any time."

The boy took the key reluctantly, but he nodded. "I do," he said. "I can unlock and come out after dark?"

"Be careful, little ones." She touched each upturned face then ran for the stairs.

When the Fa-kichwa found her she was sitting in the women's rooms working on a piece of embroidery. Hodarzu was playing quietly across the room with S'kiliza, and Mara was sitting at her knees. He stood in the doorway and beckoned to her. Kitosime silently laid her embroidery aside and walked across the room to him. He drew her into the hallway. "We burn a fire at dawn. You will come?"

She lowered her eyes. "I should not, Fa-kichwa. I am woman."

"Lady, Kobe would approve it. You are his blood. You will come." His hands stroked her arms, sweaty and shaking, pulling her closer and closer to him until she was pressed against his body. He was trembling, febrile with excitement. She could feel his arousal and stood very still, caught in a paralysis of horror. He was panting, his breath hot on her face. Then he pushed her away. "Be there," he said hoarsely, then wheeled and strode off toward the front of the house.

Kitosime staggered to the door and stood with her forehead pressed against the wood. Her stomach churned. No more delay. He was going to make her eat wilding flesh, then he would. . . . She closed her fingers around the eyestones and tried to laugh. But the sound frightened her with its unsteady shrillness. She pressed her back against the door until her shaking stopped.

When she stepped inside the room again, Mara sat staring at her. S'kiliza was smothering Hodarzu's disturbed cries against her meager breast. Kitosime projected a calm determination that brought startled reactions from all three. Hodarzu stopped crying, wriggled from S'kiliza and trotted over to her. She scooped him up and carried him to her chair. S'kiliza came to sit beside Mara and both girls stared up at her.

"The boys and I," she began, then stopped as protests came from both girls. She laughed, relaxed, low and easy. She touched Mara's cheek. "I learn slowly, don't I. Very well. All

of us, we'll have to . . . to kill the Fa-men. Tonight." She
closed her eyes. "We'll stay in my room until time. The door
bars. Skik, would you stay with. . . ." She felt the girl's em-
phatic negation and smiled. "I didn't think so. We'll leave
Hodarzu there, though. He's too little to understand and
might make noise." She was tired. After the tension and
terror in the hall, she felt weak and boneless. At the moment she wondered if she could even stand. "In a little
while," she murmured. "In a little while."

Kitosime knelt by the railings, straining past the cistern to
see the field dimly visible behind the barn. The Umgovi cluster was up again, its deceptive silver light giving the illusion
of great clarity. Shadowy figures moved about a growing
heap in the field. *Two*, she thought. But she couldn't be sure.
Fireman of course, he had to build the fire. The other? Or
others?

"How many do you see?" she whispered to Cheo.

"Two." He pressed his face against the railing. "One make
fire. One jump around like he crazy."

Some kind of rite, she thought. *The others must be in the
barn with the children. Fa-kichwa and Sniffer.* She shivered.
*Has to be them, places they wouldn't give up, tormenting the
children.* Small hands stroked her shoulders, her children projected COMFORT. She sighed. "The rest of you, do you see
only two?" When they nodded, she said, "I too. But I had to
be sure." She frowned at the shadows, feeling a great uncertainty and a greater need. "We have no weapons."

In the darkness beside her Amea hissed, then said,
"Kitchen have knife, mama 'Tosime. We get one of the Fa-
beasts alone, we cut him throat." The longest speech he'd
made since he'd come. Kitosime could feel the effort behind
it.

"He's a man. Strong."

"He one man," Cheo said fiercely. "We six and you. He
hurt us, so be. But we get him dead. Dead!"

"I know so little." Kitosime rubbed her aching eyes. "Just
that we don't dare fail." She felt their agreement and determination. "One at a time," she whispered.

The night was suddenly lighter. Kitosime scurried on her
hands and knees along the roofwalk to the eastern side. The
glow was fading but whiteness like a ghost veil hung over the

peaks. She watched until the children's impatience brought
her back to herself.

"What that?" Wame wriggled beside her and stared at the
remnants of the glow.

"I think it means Haribu is dead. Manoreh and the
Hunters have finished their job. I wish he was here."

"He?"

She smiled at the jealousy obvious in the children's reaction. "Manoreh. My husband. He's a Ranger."

"Don't need him, you got us." Wame took hold of her
wrist and shook her arm, radiating a deep and bitter jealousy.
Kitosime looked at the others and sensed the same thing in
them. "My dears. . . ." She turned helplessly from one to
the other. "Oh, Meme Kalamah, there isn't time." She
crawled through the children to the stairs, keeping below the
railing so her silhouette wouldn't show to the men in the
field. "Come," she said softly. "We can talk about this later.
Now we have to deal with the Fa-men." She went down the
stairs, straightening up until she was once more walking erect.
The children followed silently behind.

Kitosime slipped into the barn and stood watching the Fa-
men in the great hay storage vault. Sniffer was prancing
about the huddled wilding children, jabbing at them with the
assegai, his shrill, unlovely voice raised in a wailing chant.
Fa-kichwa sat a little apart, a small drum resting on his
crossed legs. He was beating out the chant rhythm. In the
feeble lamplight she could see that several children were
bleeding and all of them were numb with terror, glassy-eyed,
slack mouthed, slumped over. She closed her eyes, closed her
hands into fists, summoned her courage. Then she arranged
her features into her doll mask and stepped gracefully into
the light. She moved in a gentle, swaying walk to stand in
front of the Fa-kichwa, one hand stretched out to him. "I
have come," she murmured.

Fa-kichwa frowned. "You come too early, lady. Go back
to the house and wait."

She went to her knees with a serpentine movement that
brought sweat to his face. He'd kept his hands moving on the
drum, but now the beat faltered. "Must I?" she said softly.
"The dark frightens me."

He rested his hand on the drumhead. "You came."

"In fear. I can't go back, not alone." Her breathing stilled.

Would he tell her to stay or would he escort her back? Which was stronger, his fanaticism or his lust? She dropped her eyes modestly, bowed her head before him, displaying the gentle curve of her long neck.

The kichwa glanced at Sniffer. Then he stood. "Continue," he said sternly. "I will return in a few minutes."

Kitosime watched Sniffer from the corner of her eye, wondering if he would protest. But he shrugged and took up the chant again. Fa-kichwa thrust a hand at her. "Come."

The walk back to the house was a nightmare. His hands moved over her body. His breathing was hoarse and rapid by the time they reached the kitchen. Fa-men were supposed to remain celibate before a fire but he'd forgotten everything beyond wanting her. He pushed her through the kitchen door and into the room that was lit by a single lamp and filled with swaying shadows. Kitosime started toward the door into the main house but he stopped her. "Here," he said hoarsely. He pulled the broochpin from the rollknot of her dresscloth, pulled the cloth away from her body and tossed it to one side. Then he was on her, pushing her down, squeezing her breasts, mouth slobbering over her, kneeing her legs apart.

Cheo came out of the shadows and drove the butcher knife into his back. It went completely through the Fa-kichwa and scratched Kitosime between her ribs. Lost in a hurricane of blindrage, Cheo jerked the knife out and stabbed again and again, until Amea and the others pulled him off.

Kitosime shoved Fa-kichwa's body off her and sat up, gasping and nauseated. She wiped absently at the trickle of blood, then huddled on her knees vomiting until she was shivering with exhaustion. Then Mara was beside her with a cool wet cloth. The girl bathed Kitosime's face and helped her to sit up. Between them, the two girls sponged the blood and stains from the woman's trembling body. Kitosime gradually stopped shaking. She looked into the anxious eyes and smiled, projected APPRECIATION/LOVE. She stood and took the dresscloth from Mara, twisted the rollknot into place. She looked around vaguely. "Anyone seen my broochpin?" S'kiliza shook her head and crawled about the floor looking for it.

Kitosime went to the silent boys. She folded Cheo in her arms and held his trembling body close for a long time. "You saved me from a terrible thing," she said softly. "Thank you." She examined the others. "You all right?"

Amea shrugged. Wame nodded. Liado said nothing, just stood shivering, eyes wild. Kitosime brushed her hand across her face. Worse than she'd expected. The killing had disturbed them deeply. With light touches she projected COM-FORT/LOVE/GOOD/ACCEPTANCE and stroked them until some of the dark mood was gone. Liado leaned against her, relaxed now and heavy. She turned to the girls. "You could stay here."

Mara scowled. "No," she said and looked for support to S'kiliza. S'kiliza sat up and shook her head. "We come," she said.

"It's the Sniffer in the barn."

"And wildings." Mara smiled fiercely. "I go."

"No!" Kitosime thrust out a hand. "Mara. . . ."

"No. What you do, mama 'Tosime, I do." She lifted her chin and marched out of the kitchen. Kitosime snatched her broochpin from S'kiliza and ran after her, jabbing the pin through the rollknot as she ran.

Cheo growled, swept the others with angry eyes, then ran out with them following on his heels.

When Mara slipped into the barn, Sniffer was squatting beside the abandoned drum, eyes fixed on the dazed wildings. "Fa-kichwa say you come," she gasped out. "Wildings. In the garden. He got, but need help." She stood panting, a slender immature figure in her simple dresscloth, obviously excited. One glance at the wildings reassured Sniffer. They weren't going anywhere. He limped over to Mara, his short leg dragging badly.

"Where?" he shrilled.

"Follow." She ran out.

When he plunged through the door, he tripped over S'kiliza crouched in front of the opening. Then the boys were on him. The knives flashed and he was quickly as dead as the Fa-kichwa. Kitosime came out of the shadows projecting CALM/QUIET/PEACE to damp the excitement, rage and terror surging through the children. She went from one to the other, stroking them, touching, patting, soothing. She was hating this. More and more she saw how the killing was hurting the children. Especially the older boys. She hugged Amea a long time, loving him, approving him, soothing the violent emotions that were tearing him apart, then did the same for Cheo.

When the children were finally calmed, she led them into the barn.

The wildings had begun to recover from their terror trance. They stopped working at the neck rope when they sensed the newcomers, stiffening again with fear.

Kitosime stopped. "Cheo," she whispered. "Amea. Cut off that rope. Wame, the rest of you. Calm them. Don't let them run out of here in panic. Though the hounds are tied up in the courtyard, there are two Fa-men left out there." She nodded toward the back of the barn.

With the resilience of youth, the boys grinned as they ran to free the wildings. The bloody knives cut the rope from their necks. Once free, the boys fluttered about in the swift fluid communing of the wildings.

Kitosime leaned against one of the supports. *Two more Fa-men. Do we have to kill them too? These are children, they shouldn't have to kill men.* She swung around against the wood, ignoring the prick of splinters stabbing into her skin. She knew the other two Fa-men had to die. *We live or they live,* she thought. *I wish. . . .* She touched the eye-stones. *Manoreh, Manoreh, I begin to see why you couldn't bear to stay here. But I wish you were here now. If the boys have to kill again. . . .*

She moved back to the children. The new wildings were seated in a tight half circle. They were five boys, blood drying on their dirty hides. They stared at her, still wary of adults.

"Cheo, will they stay? They can go if they are careful, do they know that?"

"They know. Know too it better to stay. We kill Fa-men and they safe. Fa-men run them long time. They have three girls with them, but make girls go off. This one. . . ." Cheo pointed to a painfully thin boy with great luminous eyes. "He very strong FEELER. He say girls, they come after, are close." Cheo grinned. "He surprised that we talk." His pride swelled.

With an amused snort, Kitosime pinched his ear. "Should have named you Big-man-who-talks-too-much," she murmured. Then she frowned at the wildings, wondering what to do with them. "We need some way to pull the other Fa-men in here. One at a time."

S'kiliza tugged at her arm. "My turn," she said. "I tell one that Fa-kichwa want him in here. Just like Mara. When he come in. . . ." She jerked her hand up and down.

While Kitosime was trying to decide what had to be done, she heard a keening whine that passed over the barn and swooped down until it sounded as if it was right outside. She wheeled to face the door, vibrating to a touch that was unbelievably familiar, unbelievably welcome.

Manoreh stood in the door, Faiseh behind him. Then he stepped inside, smiling at her.

When the night turned bright as day, Umeme nearly dropped the waterskin he and Havih had just filled at the trough in the stable's corral. He grabbed Havih and dropped flat, then crawled for the inky shadow at the end of the stable. The two boys pressed themselves against the wall and peered at the fading flare hanging above the eastern mountain peaks.

Havih nudged Umeme. "What's that?"

"Don't know." Umeme frowned thoughtfully. "Here." He thrust the waterskin at Havih. "Take this up into the loft and make sure the rest keep quiet. I'm going on the roof to take a look."

He waited until Havih had slipped around the corner, then began climbing the extended edges of the wall. As he flipped onto the roof, he saw two Chwerevamen trot past, heading for the nearest energy gun. He frowned, wondered if that might cause problems for him and the other boys. After a minute he began working his way along the roof then up the shingles to the peak. At the top he looked around.

The last traces of the flare were washed into a faint cloud behind the mountains. He blinked, vaguely disturbed. There was a calm in the air that bothered him until he noticed the absence of the shrill, intermittent hum from the psi-screen. He examined the screen more closely. No more pulsing flickers. Then he strained toward the hare ring. For a moment he saw no change, then a hare staggered and collapsed against another already stretched out stiff on the ground. *They're dead*, he thought. *The Hunters did it. They're dead*.

He heard a growing murmur as the streets began to fill. Beneath him Chwereva compound was stirring. There were men now at each of the four guns. Hastily he slid down the roof, flipped over the edge, and half fell down the side of the stable to the ground. He hesitated in the shadow as several Chwerevamen trotted past, heading for the front gate, then he darted around the corner and through the small side door.

In the loft he found the boys steaming with curiosity. The concentrated emotion almost flattened him. "Hey," he hissed. "Let me breathe." He climbed onto a mound of hay. "Hares are dead. Or almost," he said. As they leaped up, mouths open, he glared at them. "Quiet! We aren't out of this yet. We're all that's left of the Tembeat. You want to see the Director's death wasted. Or the teachers'?" When they calmed down, he said, "Havih, what's our first goal?"

"Sneak over the wall, get out of the city, steal a boat." Havih grinned, and bowed to them all.

"Anrah, what's next?"

"We sail to the coast, then out to the islands. We pick an island where not too many people are."

"Ketreh?"

"Find a place with water and maybe a house, or build a house. Start the Tembeat again."

Umeme could feel their excitement rising. He projected CALM/ASSURANCE as best he could and when they quieted, said, "All right. Get your stuff. Havih, take care of the ropes. Ketreh, help him. We got to get out of here now. Kiwanji's waking up. Especially we got to get over the wall fast and quiet. Don't want the Chwerevamen to get after us with those guns. We go over near where the cistern is. Some shadow there. Got it? Good. Five minutes. Let's go."

The line of boys slipped rapidly down the doubled rope, jerked it loose, then drifted through the clots of men, unnoticed in the growing confusion. They wound quickly through the streets, working toward the western side of the city where the river curved past.

A shout broke through the confused noise of the streets. At first it was a jumble of sound, then men came running into the center of the city yelling excitedly, "The hares. The hares are dead. The hares are dead! THE HARES ARE DEAD!"

The boys leaped over the low wall and ran for the river, moving along the riverside piers, scanning the boats tied up there. Most were the great flat-bottomed barges that had brought the clans here from the holdings, but here and there they saw smaller boats, ranging from one-man rowboats to more elaborate day-sailers. Umeme stopped beside a neat eight-meter craft. "This is good," he said. "Climb in. Havih, you pick out two to help and get the sail set. I'll take the tiller for the first bit. The rest of you, haul your gear in and get yourselves stowed." He stepped over the side quickly and sat beside the tiller, while the boys scurried.

They had the sail up in a few minutes. The boat was a little crowded with the fifteen boys and all their gear, but they paid no attention to discomfort, laughing and joking, released at last from their enforced silence. Umeme smiled, feeling the same release from tension, but being in charge, he couldn't let down too much. Ketreh flopped down beside him, the boom sheet in one hand. "We're ready," he said. ·

"Wait a minute." Havih jumped onto the rough dock and darted up the slope. He came back almost immediately, a hare body dangling from his hand. "Wanted to see what killed 'em," he gasped. He tumbled into the boat, rocking it precariously, then crawled back to Umeme.

Umeme grunted. "Time to go. Qareh, get the bow line. Lerzu, the one by your elbow. Ketreh, pay out that sheet a little so the sail can catch some air."

The boat eased out to the middle of the river, the sail filling, beginning to drive them along like a bird skimming over the water. In a few minutes Kiwanji vanished behind the bank and the trees. The massive kuumti trees of the river valley began to rise higher and higher until their wide branches left only a narrow space over the center of the Mungivir.

Havih turned the hare over and over in his hands then touched the clotted fur around the eyes and nostrils. "Look." He showed the hare's head to Umeme. "Blood came out the nose and mouth, even out around the eyes. Something sure blew their brains."

"Hunters." Umeme wrinkled his nose at the hare. "Get rid of that thing, huh?"

Havih tossed the hare into the river and wiped his hands on his shorts. "How long to the coast, you think?"

"Depends on wind. With a good breeze, two, three days; current alone, maybe five. According to Agoteh, the river's good and deep the whole way, no shallows to worry about. So we got it made. Until we get to the coast, anyway. Agoteh said we got to watch out. People there are weird. And no laws or customs to keep them straight." He frowned at the boys lounging along the boat in front of him. "Anyway, we got a few days of peace."

Faiseh was behind the dais that held the body of the watuk and the shattered egg. Two more bodies were sprawled beside him. He held one energy gun. A second lay by his knee. Across the great cavern watuk guards were crouched in the corridor arch. Several of their company were scattered on the metacrete outside the corridor. As Aleytys and Grey stepped from the lift, one of the guards leaned out and shot at Faiseh. The Ranger ducked behind the dais, then returned fire. Both shots missed and the two sides continued to watch each other closely.

Grey shoved past Aleytys and ran to the dais, dropping behind it just in time to avoid a burst of energy from the arch. Faiseh grunted with satisfaction as the guard toppled slowly out onto the metacrete. He grinned at Grey. "Want to do that again? You're a great decoy."

"Sorry. Any idea how many of them in there?"

"I touch half a dozen. Could be a few more." He glanced back at Aleytys crouched inside the lift. "We're kind of stuck here. What about her? Can she do something? We got to get Manoreh out of the lab. If he's still alive."

"He's alive." Grey tapped the spare energy gun. "If we keep their heads down, Lee can fetch him." He took the gun and looked around one end of the dais. Faiseh wriggled about so he could cover the other end. Grey got comfortable, then called, "Get over here, Lee. Keep down and come fast."

When she reached them, two more guards were stretched out on the floor and she had a long singe on her back. Grey started to speak, but she held up a hand. "Give me a minute." She grimaced. "Sore as hell." She touched her seared buttocks. "Should keep my rear down." She closed her eyes. Faiseh gasped as the charred flesh smoothed over. In a moment all trace of the burn wound was gone. She opened her eyes and smiled. "So. What now?"

"Manoreh's in the lab still. If we keep them pinned, think you can get him?"

She measured the distance from the dais to the lab arch. "He's unconscious," she said slowly. Then she grinned at Grey. "Do a better job of keeping their heads down this time. I'm running out of juice."

"Only our best." He lifted an eyebrow. Faiseh nodded. "We're set, Lee. Go!"

She was up and away, running in irregular spurts and arcs, the green dress flaring up about her thighs and swirling about them in a flow of emerald, her red hair swinging and dancing as she dipped and darted. Grey and Faiseh kept the guards occupied, and she reached the arch untouched, then vanished inside.

The two men waited, snapping occasional bursts at the arch as guards grew curious or restless or tried to get off a shot. With two of them firing, more often than not, the guard tumbled out. Grey checked his meter. About a quarter charge. He edged his head around. "How much you got left?"

"Not a hell of a lot. What's holding her up?"

Grey shook his head. "No idea. Look, there can't be that many of them left."

"I touch two."

"So." Grey put the energy gun on the floor and slid it across to Faiseh. "Keep them honest. I'm going in to see what the problem is."

"There were guards in the lab too."

Grey snapped his fingers. "I'm not disarmed, friend. Head up. I'm off." He dashed from the dais, heard the soft whine of the gun, but made the lab with nothing more than a charred spot on the sleeve of his tunic.

Manoreh was stretched out unconscious on a black-padded table. The straps that had secured him were dangling at its side. Aleytys bent over him, her hands flattened against his chest. His hands were closed around her wrists. Her face was frozen in shock. His body was arched slightly under her hands, the same shock was on his face.

"Lee?" He touched her cheek. Her flesh was stone-hard. Cold. Her arm wouldn't move. He tried to pry Manoreh's fingers loose but the flesh seemed glued to Aleytys's arm.

He stepped back. Some complication of that link between them. *Break the link.* He looked down at his stunner fingers. *Manoreh first.* He slid his hand along Manoreh's shoulder and worked it up under the metal helmet—badly discolored but still on the Ranger's head. He jerked the helmet off and threw it across the room, then placed his fingers under the curve of the Ranger's skull. He gave the watuk two jolts from the stunner, stood back and waited. Nothing seemed to happen. He touched Aleytys's face. Still frozen. "Try again," he muttered. "Now you." He slipped his hand under her hair, stroked the curve of her neck. "Hope this works, love." He activated the stunners twice again.

For a moment the tableau held, then Aleytys's stiff form melted. Grey caught her and lifted her away from the table.

Leaving her stretched out against the wall, he searched among the dead and unconscious bodies in the bloody debris on the floor and found several energy guns. He checked the charges, grunted with satisfaction, then stripped a weapon belt from a guard's body and strapped it on. He tucked all but one of the guns behind the belt, then moved to the arch. He waited until he got Faiseh's attention, pointing along the wall toward the corridor's arch. Then he slipped out and ran noiselessly along the wall. Before the last guard had time to react he was facing the gun in Grey's hand. He walked out of the arch, resignation and fear blending in his face.

Faiseh came toward them. "That's all," he said.

Grey rubbed his nose. "You can tell if a man is lying?"

"Most times. Why?"

Grey turned to the guard. "How many more guards in this place?"

The boy swallowed. He was much younger than the other guards. His silver-green skin dulled to a dirty olive. "Haribu." His indigo eyes searched their faces. "Not many. Don't know for sure. Two or three working on a skimmer in the port. Up there."

When Faiseh nodded, Grey said, "Good enough." He directed the shivering guard to the cage in the middle of the cavern. The guard crawled inside and stood holding the bars, watching forlornly as the Ranger and the Hunter went back through the lab arch.

Faiseh was surprised to see the two unconscious figures. "What happened?"

"The link. They were tied together. I had to stun both of them to pry them apart. Think you can carry him?"

"Why not." Faiseh crossed to the table.

Grey knelt beside Aleytys. She was still out, would be out for a while yet. He lifted her onto his shoulder, then went quickly through the arch and trotted for the lift.

With Aleytys huddled in one corner of the lift and Manoreh across from her, Grey shut the door and touched the sensor square that would take them to the Vryhh's nest. "We've got one stop to make. To pick up Haribu."

"Ah!" Faiseh looked down at Aleytys. "Remarkable woman."

Grey smiled down at her. "Very."

The lift stopped. "Wait here. Be back in a minute." He stepped through the doorway into the bedroom. The chair was empty. He crossed to the fresher, its door gaping open. Empty. He came back to the center of the room. "Damn," he said mildly. "Damn." Shaking his head, he went back to the lift.

Faiseh questioned. "Haribu?"

"Crawled under a rock somewhere. Let's get out of here."

This time the lift opened into another cavern floored with metacrete. One end was open to the night air. Several skimmers were scattered about. Two men were bending over the engine of one of them. They looked up as the lift opened. Grey's gun fired before they could move. They dropped without a word. Dead.

Grey stepped out of the lift and pointed to the skimmer nearest the open port. "Get those two inside and wait for me."

He walked through flurries of dust, stirred up by gusts of wind coming in through the opening in the side of the mountain. He glanced toward the portal and nodded. *The Vryhh*, he thought. *Got out of here without looking behind.* He grinned and stepped over the sprawled watuk. *Lee must have scared hell out of him.*

Using the tools left by the dead mechanics, he worked over three of the skimmers, then swung inside each and started the motors. Instead of the smooth hum, there was a tooth-jarring whine that pulsed like the breathing of a lung-shot beast. He stretched his mouth in a feral grin. Ten minutes and they'd blow.

Hastily he jumped back to the metacrete and ran to the skimmer by the portal. Still smiling grimly, he sent the skimmer darting out of the mountain, forcing it into maximum climb. He didn't relax until they were out of the mountains and cruising over the valley floor.

Faiseh looked back at the mountains. "What's the hurry?"

Grey leaned back. "Ever see what happens when a skimmer engine overloads?"

Faiseh grunted. "Not likely."

"Watch the mountains then. Should be happening about now."

As he spoke there was a great flare of light. The polarizing glass of the viewports went solid black for a moment, then returned to transparency as the flare faded to a white veil whose glow diminished as they watched. A moment later the skimmer rocked as a blast of air caught it, but the stabilizers leveled it.

"Right," Faiseh said. He drummed his fingers on the console. "Doesn't make riding in this very comfortable right now."

"Relax. Safe enough."

"Where we heading?"

"Kiwanji."

"A favor?"

"Why not. What is it?"

"Drop Manoreh and me at Kobe's Holding first?"

"No problem." He sat up and swung the skimmer around until it was moving south and west, heading toward Kobe's Holding.

Some minutes later Manoreh groaned and sat up. Rubbing at his numbed arms and legs, he muttered, "What happened?"

Faiseh chuckled, repeating what he knew of events since the egg exploded. "Look back," he finished. "You can still see the cloud shining a little." He grinned. "Glad to see you taking notice. You weigh a ton."

Manoreh started to laugh then groaned. "My head feels like you been stomping on it, couz."

Aleytys stirred, moaned softly. Manoreh reached for her, but Faiseh caught his hand. "Huh-uh, couz. Bad idea."

Manoreh looked down at Aleytys. "I see."

Aleytys sat up, rubbed at her eyes, twisted her head back and forth, until she straightened and met Grey's eyes.

He swung his chair around and took her hand. "You all right?"

"In one piece, more or less." She rubbed the back of her head. "You stunned me?"

"Had to." She looked tired but relaxed. He was reluctant to disturb her hard-won peace, but she had to know of the Vryhh's escape. He spoke to stop the question he saw forming on her face. "I set three skimmers to overload. Blew the place to dust." He pointed at the cloud still visible through the back viewports. She glanced back, nodded; then she began looking around the skimmer, frowning. Grey leaned back, waiting for her to ask about the Vryhh.

Faiseh touched his shoulder. "Kobe's Holding coming up," he said and pointed down.

Relieved, Grey swung the chair around and took back the

controls. He brought the skimmer around and set it down in the flat space between the barn and the kitchen garden. Then he looked from Manoreh to Faiseh. "Our business is finished," he said crisply.

"Grey. . . ." Aleytys touched his arm.

He shook his head. "Finished, Lee." He tapped a sensor and the door beside Faiseh slid open. "Sorry to shove you out, Rangers, but we're due in Kiwanji."

"Got you." Faiseh jumped down quickly and stood waiting for Manoreh.

Manoreh rubbed at the back of his neck. "Aleytys, I. . . ."

She smiled. "No need. I know."

He eased to his feet and stood bent over, his shoulders pressed against the top of the skimmer. "You've certainly shaken loose a lot of my ideas." He dropped from the skimmer and stood watching while she came to kneel in the doorway. "Kitosime will thank you. As for me, I'll wait and see."

Aleytys laughed. "I wish I could stay and watch, but. . . ." She shrugged.

"Not a good idea. I've got problems enough with one independent lady." He pointed to the barn. "Who waits there." With Faiseh he started for the barn.

Aleytys leaned out the door, her body tensing, then she wriggled around and slid into the seat beside Grey. "There's a dead man by that door. Grey. . . ."

The door beside her slid shut with a crisp finality and Grey took the skimmer up, sending it toward Kiwanji.

Chapter XVI

★ ★ ★ ★ ★ ★ ★

With Faiseh close behind, Manoreh pushed open the small door and stepped into the barn. A rush of gladness made him blink until he realized that Kitosime was projecting with a power that nearly suffocated him. He heard Faiseh suck in his breath. A dead man, hacked to pieces outside, now this.

He looked past her. In the shadows at the edge of the light five wilding boys hovered, ready to run or fight. They were dirty, ragged, covered with small cuts and crusted blood. He projected REASSURANCE/CALM. Then turned back to Kitosime.

She's magnificent, he thought. Her head was up, the feeble light from the lamp striking silver highlights from her high cheekbones and sinking her eyes into deep shadow. She burned with pride and defiance now that her first flush of joy had dissipated. Two girls pressed against her, one on each side, sharing in her defiance, slightly jealous. *Wildings*, he thought, startled. But they were neat and clean in their dress-cloths, their hair combed into tight knots. Four boys stood by her, watching him with hostility. *Wildings. Had to be, the way they projected emotion.* Manoreh frowned at one of the smaller boys. He looked familiar. Then he remembered. *The boy who'd scooped up the dead hares. He's changed. Meme Kalamah, he's changed. Wildings. Neat and clean in tunic and shorts. Kitosime. . . .* He smiled. "You've been busy, Kitosime." He projected AMUSEMENT/APPRECIATION/WONDER.

"Very." She was making no concessions. After a moment's strained silence, she said, "And you?"

"The world is saved."

That startled a laugh from her. She relaxed a little, rested arms lightly around the girls' shoulders. "I haven't done so badly either." She smiled. "Welcome home, husband. And meet our new children."

157

Manoreh laughed. "With pleasure. They have names?"

"Oh yes, indeed. They find names very important." She smiled proudly at the children. "The two big boys are Amea and Cheo. They have fought well for us. Wame there," she pointed, "he's our story teller. And Liado—" she indicated the silent staring boy next to Wame. "He's our ears and eyes." She touched Mara's cheek. "This is Mara. She escaped from a clan Bighouse and survived in the Wild for five years. And this little imp is S'kiliza." She hugged S'kiliza.

Manoreh took a step forward. It was absurd to be standing here, talking at each other. So close, yet so far apart. *There's six months between us,* he thought. *And three years' blindness on my part.* He was aware of Faiseh fidgeting behind him. *He's wondering what the fuss is about, why I let her defy me.* He tried to shake off his malaise. He took another step toward Kitosime, projected QUESTION?

With a shake of her head, she denied him an answer. There were silver highlights on her face and her hoop earrings brushed her neck. She was achingly lovely. He felt a surge of desire, but repressed it. Wrong time and place. His eyes dropped to the girl beside her. *Mara,* he thought. *How does she know about Mara?* He lifted his head. "How do you know about her?"

Kitosime looked startled. "She told me."

"You taught her to speak?"

"Yes." She frowned, projected CONFUSION. "Not really. I just helped her remember what she already knew. They all spoke before they went wild." She smiled at her small satellites and got back from them a wave of possessive affection, then she faced Manoreh again. "There are some things that *need* words."

"Do you have any idea what you've done, love?" He laughed, the sound booming in the great vault. "You've made yourself a Tembeat."

"No!" She scowled. "Nothing like that thing."

"Exactly like that thing. What do your think they did with us, the boys they brought in?"

"Then why so few!" She was abruptly very angry, and glared at him out of shadowed eyes. "There are hundreds of wildings out there." She flung out a hand encompassing the Sawasawa. He could feel the energy snapping in her, the power. "You men! You let them run loose, dirty, hungry, in constant danger of being burned and eaten by Fa-men. And you took in no girls at all. Why?" She was breathing quickly. Under the rollknot her breasts rose and fell.

Manoreh shook his head. "I was wrong," he said quietly. "Not exactly like the Tembeat."

"Wrong!" She spat the word at him.

"You've done more than the Tembeat thought of doing. Until now. . . ." he said, as she snorted impatiently. "Until now," he repeated, "no one knew it was possible to reclaim those already wild. All the men and boys at the Tembeat came there still speaking. Their clans sent them as a last desperate measure to keep them from the wild. We didn't know. . . ." He was silent a minute. "Do you think we had more freedom than anyone else? Everything the Director did, he did on sufferance. The Holders. . . ." He shrugged. "They tolerated us, that's all. Kitosime. . . ." He reached toward her. "Do you see what you've done?" He laughed suddenly. "You've changed our world more wildly than. . . ." As he saw the possibilities, excitement kindled in him. "Do you see?"

She ran to him and put her hands in his. "You understand," she cried. "I never expected you to understand."

He kissed her hand. "Don't remind me what a fool I've been, love. Forgive?"

With a sob of excitement and joy, she pressed against him, forgetting her anger, her fears, even the children.

Faiseh grunted with embarrassment and wandered toward the back of the barn. Suddenly, he stood rigid, facing into the darkness, then he came running back. He slapped Manoreh on the shoulder. "Trouble, couz!"

Manoreh scowled down at him, irritated. "What?" he snapped.

"I touch two outside. Bothered about something, they are. And coming toward the barn."

"Fa-men," Kitosime gasped. "There were two of them left, the ones making the Fa-fire out there." She pointed into the darkness.

Manoreh put her gently aside. "Keep the children quiet. Faiseh, where. . . ." He probed the darkness. "Ah, I see. Think they saw the skimmer?"

Faiseh shrugged. "Been in here before if they had, I'd say. You're better'n me at FEELING. What do you think? Any urgency?"

Manoreh probed further, then shook his head, grimacing with distaste. "Just hungry and a bit bothered about something." He rubbed at the back of his neck. "Must be getting toward dawn. Coming for the wildings, I think. Wondering why the others haven't brought them out."

"Right." Faiseh stroked the butt of the energy gun. "We wait here or go get them?"

"Here, I think. You?"

"Here." He kicked at the straw. "Good enough."

Manoreh touched Kitosime's shoulder. "Get the children out of sight. Flat on their stomachs. You too."

Kitosime nodded. She moved quickly to the scowling children, ignoring hostility and jealousy. "Cheo, Amea, help me. Get everyone over there behind the hay. Hurry."

Urged by the oldest boys, the children melted into the darkness. Kitosime hesitated, looked back at the two men standing close beside the flickering lamp. "Manoreh, what about you?"

"Get down." Unsnapping his holster flap, he drew out the energy gun. "They haven't a hope, Kita. Now get down, will you!"

Kitosime stretched out beside Liado, waiting and watching anxiously. After a minute she felt the boy trembling against her. She stroked his back with a comforting hand, feeling the shaking slowly diminish. She smiled. *Could use a little stroking myself.*

The sliding door on the far side of the barn squealed and rumbled open. She heard a low mumble of voices, then the Second called, "Kichwa?" She edged closer to the hay and peered around it. Manoreh and Faiseh stood quietly in the middle of the circle of lamplight, relaxed, guns held loosely. The Fa-men's footsteps came closer, then Second knocked open a stanchion and stepped through into the hay vault. "Sniffer?"

Manoreh waited, watching the shadowy figure. He saw the figure stiffen. Second hissed and swung his assegai back for a quick cast. Beside him, the Fireman howled and leaped clear, his spear back and ready.

Faiseh and Manoreh leveled the energy guns. The guns flared once in narrow bursts of light, thin as one of the stalks of straw under their feet.

Faiseh strolled over to the bodies and flipped one onto its

back. "Heart shot." He tapped his gun against his jaw. "Not realy fair, guns against spears."

Manoreh slid his gun back and snapped the holster shut. "Fa-men," he said, his voice contemptuous. "Died too easy." He helped Kitosime to her feet.

Cheo slipped past her and trotted to Faiseh's side. He touched the gun, projecting AWE/DESIRE, then scowled down at the bodies. He kicked at the Second, kicked again.

Faiseh rested a hand on his shoulder. "Easy, boy." He tightened his grip as Cheo tried to twist away. "Pull up, cub. You're too big to act like a baby." The Ranger smiled down at the boy, projecting CALMNESS/AMUSEMENT. Cheo stopped struggling. In a minute he smiled back. Faiseh cuffed him lightly, then walked back into the lamplight. "What now?"

"Out of here." Manoreh hesitated. The wilding boys were sidling out of the shadows, eyes on the guns, forgetting their hostility in their fascination with the weapons. The girls hung behind but they too kept their eyes on the holsters. Amea edged cautiously up to Manoreh. He reached out and touched the bit of gunbutt still visible. "Is more? For us?"

Manoreh laughed, but shook his head. "Not like these." He faced Faiseh. "Kobe has an armory in his sitting room. Should be some guns left there, couz."

Faiseh grinned at the eager faces. "Should be enough to put darters in these hands. Then let the Fa-men come."

"No!" Kitosime pulled Manoreh around. "No, Manoreh. They're children."

Anger at her presumption flared to blindrage; he lifted his hand, fighting the rage back until he stood sick and shaking, sweat rolling down his face. He thrust out a shaking hand and she took it, gave him back UNDERSTANDING/LOVE. Then he was able to smile at her. "Give me time, Kita. One doesn't change old habits in a day."

She nodded. "I won't go back, Manoreh. I won't be a doll again. I can't." Faiseh and the children waited quietly, not sure what was happening but aware that it was important. Kitosime struggled for words. "Just talk to me," she said slowly. "Just remember I'm there. Listen to me sometimes. . . ." Her voice trailed off.

He touched her cheek, then took her hand. "Kita, about the guns. No, don't back off, let me explain. Wherever we go, there'll be people who'll want what we have or try to kill us."

"I suppose so. It's just . . . I hate the idea of the children killing again. It hurt them, Manoreh. You don't know. You weren't there. It hurt them."

"I saw the Sniffer's body. A knife?"

She nodded.

"Kita," he said slowly, "there's a big difference between using a knife to slash a man to death and putting a dart in him. A matter of distance. There isn't the same shock. You don't feel the dart going in. We'll all be safer if the boys are armed. Can you see that?"

She nodded. "Not just the boys," she said firmly. "The girls should be armed and taught. And me." She scanned his startled face. "If more guns mean more safety, then arm us too. Or don't you think we can learn to use them?"

Manoreh chuckled. "No you don't, Kita, I won't touch that. You get your guns. Just prove you can handle them."

She snorted. "As well as the boys. Bet you."

Faiseh groaned. "Don't do that, Kitosime. He always wins."

She shook her head, laughing. "Not this time, friend." She considered Manoreh. "You've surprised me again. I thought I'd have to fight you on that."

"Watching Aleytys work was a humbling experience. The woman Hunter," he explained. "She warned me you'd be changed. Then I come back here and find you. . . ."

"What?"

"Magnificent, love. A little frightening." He rubbed at his shaved head. Small itching hairs were starting to grow, reminding him how much time was passing. "We've got to get out of here. The siege has been lifted around Kiwanji. Kobe will be back fast as he can shift the Kisima on the barges and get the walkers harnessed. And Fa-men will be chasing around. I'm damn sure more than one band came off the mountain once they saw the hares cleared off the Sawasawa. Faiseh, take some of the boys and round up all the faras you can find. We need enough to mount us all." He swept a hand around the hay vault. "And two, three more for packers."

Faiseh nodded, beckoned to Cheo and the new wildings. He strode out of the barn with the boys crowding behind him.

Manoreh smiled at the two girls and three boys still with him. "Out you go. To the house." He took Kitosime's arm and followed them. "We get the guns. And food, waterskins, clothes, ropes, anything useful we can find. We can sort it out later when we know how many packers we have. On the way, Kita, you can give me the story of your stay here. I promise to be fascinated."

Kitosime giggled and let him usher her out. Then she sobered and began a detailed account of the past few days.

Jua Churukuu was a green half-circle behind the mountains when they had the faras packed and saddled. Most of the children would have to ride bareback and the smaller ones would be riding double. Before the eastern sky had greened with dawn three wilding girls had slipped quietly into the courtyard to be greeted happily by the new boys.

Kitosime stepped out the door, feeling clumsy and uncomfortable in a tunic and shorts. She tugged at the neck thongs then at the bottoms of the shorts. When Manoreh grinned, she glared at him. "I'd like to see you try to manage a dresscloth," she snapped. His eyes twinkled. Hodarzu was sitting by his feet. The boy looked up. "Mama?"

"You see, even my own son."

Manoreh let his eyes drop to her long, slim legs. "He's not old enough yet to appreciate something good."

Kitosime gasped with indignation. "Manoreh!"

There was a sudden flurry of excitement in the courtyard. Mara ducked around a faras and came hesitantly to the foot of the steps. "Mama 'Tosime?"

Kitosime stepped to the front of the porch. "What is it, Mara? We're leaving in a few minutes."

"Mama, if there's time. . . ." Mara hesitated, then plunged on. "New wildings want names, please."

She looked down into the wildings' anxious faces. "Eight of you?" She shook her head. "That would take. . . ."

"Please, mama." S'kiliza trotted up the porch steps and tugged at Kitosime's hand. "They need names."

Manoreh chuckled. "That's telling her, Siki." He moved past Kitosime and teetered on the top step, glancing at the sun, then at the fidgeting children. "Might be a good idea, giving them names. Make them easier to keep track of." He rubbed his head. "Make it fast, love, not more than half an hour." He dropped down on the step.

"I'll try. Fool!" She laughed, settling herself beside him on the step. Hodarzu snuggled against her knees, watching the children in the court with fascination and excitement. Kitosime hugged him lightly, then called to the other children. "Mara, S'kiliza, Wame, Liado, Amea, Cheo, come here." When they were bouncing excitedly beside her, she said, "You'll have to help me."

"We help, we help." Wame grinned and beat Liado's shoulder. The others projected intense agreement. Hodarzu wiggled against Kitosime's leg and started to get up, but she tapped him on the shoulder and made him stay where he was.

She smiled proudly at them. "Good," she said. "Go and stand in front of the new ones. Come to me when I call your names, but don't let them move. We'll do that . . . um . . . three times, then I'll name the new ones. When I call the names, you say them too. Help me make them understand which name belongs with which. We have to do this fast. Understand?"

With the help of the children the naming ceremony passed very quickly. The wildings seemed to grasp the meaning of names almost at once. To Kitosime's surprise they tried to say the names she gave them. They quivered with exaltation as they stood in front of her and croaked the syllables in voices long unused. When the last child was named and had tried out her name, the whole group of children yelled hoarsely then joined in a wild dance winding through the faras and around the Mother Well, singing a fluid, silent music.

Kitosime swayed uncertainly as she jumped to her feet, then Manoreh was beside her, holding her up. "What's wrong?" he said.

"Just tired." She leaned against him, grateful for his strength. "Manoreh, the children, they're too excited. We should get them quieted down."

He wrapped his arms around her. "Rest a minute, Kita," he said softly. "Let me help. No hurry, not yet. They'll calm themselves in a minute." As she relaxed against him, he looked out at the dancing children. "Naming." There was wonder and amazement in his voice. "Something as simple as that."

Jua Churukuu was a finger's width above the mountains when they left the Holding. In minutes the long line of faras turned into the rutted road leading to the river and the ferry landing, their hooves kicking up clouds of red dust that hung in the still air a moment then fell back. Already there was a promise of breathless heat waiting for them in the afternoon. Manoreh frowned. Kitosime wasn't accustomed to riding—or the children. He watched her shifting uncomfortably in the saddle and wondered how long it would be before they had to start walking.

The ferry was a clumsy, flat-bottomed barge that moved along twin cables between landings at each side of the river, powered by heavy ropes running from the landings to drums turned by long-handled cranks. By the time Manoreh reached the beaten-hard loading space, Faiseh had stationed Cheo and Amea at the crank and was vigorously directing the loading of the faras. He looked around as Manoreh rode up. "Think we can make it in two trips, couz." Then he swung back to the ferry. "That's enough. Rahz, stand by the gate. Be ready to close it when I'm on." He led his nervous faras onto the ferry, waited till the small boy latched the gate. Then he tugged at his mustache and tilted his head to look up the bank at Manoreh. "Got a funny feeling, couz. Keep your eyes open, will you? We're kind of stuck out here. Good targets."

"Right." Manoreh waved the remaining children back behind him. Kitosime shook her head when he tried to send her with them. "Stubborn," he murmured. She laughed but shook her head again. He shrugged and pulled his gun out and held it ready, as his eyes scanned the heavy brush on the far side of the river.

Kitosime shifted again in the saddle trying to find a more comfortable position. She felt a sudden warmth on her breast, a familiar stirring. She pulled the neck pouch out and closed her fingers around it. The heat exploded, striking to the bone. She gasped and closed her eyes.

And saw fur-clad men with hideous scarred faces crouching behind heavy brush, waiting, assegais gripped in quivering hands, ready . . . saw spear tips glinting in the sun, flying into tight packed children . . . blood . . . screams . . . death. . . .

She sobbed, opened her eyes. "Manoreh. . . ."

"Don't bother me, Kita." He moved his shoulders irritably

and fixed his eyes on the other river bank. "I don't have time now."

"Time!" She flung her anger at him. "Manoreh, listen to me!"

He winced. "Dammit, Kitosime. . . ."

"Hah!" She pointed at a thick clump of brush close to the far landing. "There are Fa-men over there. Four of them." Still seething, she glared at him. "They're waiting for the ferry to come a little closer, then they're going to kill as many as they can with those cursed spears."

"How do you know?" He scowled at her, then waved her aside. "Get out of the way, will you?"

She brought the faras around, calmer now that he was listening. "The eyestones," she said.

"Ah!" He raised in the stirrups and waved vigorously. "Head down, Faiseh! Trouble!" Then he set the energy gun for continuous burn and sliced the beam through the heavy growth across the river. For a second nothing happened, then he heard screams and thrashing in the brush. He snapped off a single shot as two shadowy figures staggered up the bank. He saw one throw up its arms, but both men kept moving and vanished among the kuumti trees.

Out on the river the children were wild with excitement, blasting silent shouts of triumph at the Ranger. Faiseh shouted them into a measure of calm, then cupped his hands around his mouth and yelled, "Good shooting, couz, do the same for you some time." He swung around and started Cheo and Amea turning the crank again. The ferry began creeping forward and touched the landing a few minutes later.

Manoreh slid the gun back, snapped the holster shut. He looked thoughtfully at Kitosime. She was dusty and sweating, sitting awkwardly in the saddle, tendrils of her dark blue hair pasted around her elegant silver-green face. She was still angry, sizzling with life and energy. He eased the faras closer to her, then drew his fingers along her cheek. He pulled them away and looked down at the smear of dust and sweat on the tips. "No," he said quietly. "You won't go back to being a pretty doll."

She caught at his hand, still angry. As their eyes met, they leaned toward each other, breathing hard. Then Faiseh's yell reminded them where they were. "Tonight," Manoreh murmured.

Kitosime looked nervously around at the wide-eyed, fascinated children behind them, then at Manoreh. She sucked in a deep breath and tried to still some of the turmoil churning within her. "Tonight," she croaked. She glanced shyly at Manoreh's amused face. "I suppose I'll have to get used to people listening in."

Chapter XVII

★ ★ ★ ★ ★ ★ ★

Aleytys felt her tension flow away. Kobe's Holding was lost in the night shadows. "I feel like I'm putting down a story only half read," she murmured.

"They'll write their own ending, Lee. Without us." Grey sounded oddly somber. She turned her head and watched him lazily, wondering why he seemed so down when the Hunt was ended successfully.

"My first Hunt. Think Head will approve?" She frowned. "I wish you hadn't left the Vryhh behind. I wanted to haul him back and let Head chew on him a bit. Flames were shooting out of her ears when she told me about being tampered with." She giggled. "I've got the most godawful relatives. He said he was Tennath, my grandfather, great-grandfather, or something." She grinned at him. "You blew up a member of my family."

"Does it bother you?" He spoke with some effort. Aleytys frowned. Something was definitely bothering him.

"Not really," she said slowly. She waited a moment for him to say something more, then scanned the ground below. They were over the big river. The silver surface was broken by small black squares that looked to be pinned in place. "Barges," she said. "Holders on their way home." She paused. "I'd hate to have to live here. Maybe getting hell kicked out of them will teach them something." She sniffed. "Doubt it. Bunch of glue-brained fanatics." She smoothed her hands over the crumpled green velvet of her dress. "What's wrong, Grey?"

"I didn't blow him up, Lee. He's not dead."

"Not . . . the Vryhh?"

Grey faced her. "He wasn't in that room, Lee. Must have used another skimmer to get away while we were fetching the Rangers."

Aleytys stared at him. She was cold. COLD. There was no strength left in her. She opened her mouth to speak, produced a strangled croak, swallowed, tried again. "He knows about my son, Grey. He knows where to find him. He wants the diadem. He's gone for my son." She swallowed. "My son . . . oh god." She sagged slowly forward until her forehead rested on her knees.

Grey smoothed a hand over her hair. "Lee, we'll get the boy. I'll take you." Then he caught hold of her shoulders and lifted her until she was leaning back in the chair, gasping and coughing. He waited. Gradually her breathing steadied. "You all right, Lee?"

She passed a shaking hand across her face. "I could have killed him," she said suddenly. "I had my hand on his throat." She stared down at her hands, shuddering.

Grey caught hold of her wrists. "Don't be stupid, Lee. Stop it!"

"Or I could have just let him be. Once I flipped the power cells out of the exoskeleton, he couldn't breathe." Her voice was growing louder and shriller. She tried to free her hands from Grey's hold. "I healed him. I healed him and sent him after my son. I sent him. . . ."

Grey slapped her hard across the face. Tears flooded into her eyes. He sat back and scowled at her. "Dammit, Lee."

Aleytys closed her eyes. *Harskari*, she thought. *Help me. I need you. Shadith? My friends, I need you. What can I do? My baby. . . .* But there was nothing there, just a great echoing emptiness. The skimmer hummed steadily; she could smell a faint oiliness in the air, hear the harsh sounds of her own breathing. The tears dried on her face as emptiness expanded until she was nothing but a shell. *Oh god, how do I deal with this?* She sighed. *Nothing. There's no way . . . nothing I can do. Nothing. He could be there already in that Vryhh ship.* She raised a shaking hand and touched her lips. *Professional.* She turned her head enough to see Grey; he was a black silhouette edged in shimmers of gold. *Professional. I have a job to do. Think of that, forget Sharl and Kell the Vryhh. He won't kill my son, no, he's too crazy for that. There's time, plenty of time.* She thought of Head, the wide flashing smile, the sharp, all-seeing eyes that could twinkle one minute and pierce to bone in the next. "I owe her," she whispered. "And Grey." She sat up and rubbed her hand across her eyes. "Grey?"

He ignored her. He was leaning tautly forward, looking ahead. Aleytys watched a moment, puzzled, then followed the direction of his gaze. Kiwanji was passing below. She winced as she saw the burned-out shells of the small houses and the piles of dead hares. Then frowned as Grey left Kiwanji behind and brought the skimmer down beside his ship.

He swung the seat around. "We'll go after the boy now, if you want."

She moved uneasily in her chair. "We have to report. The fee."

"Make up your mind, Lee. I mean what I say."

She looked at the ship, then at his impassive face. For a minute she was tempted, then she shook her head. "Thanks, Grey. I . . . I know what it would cost you . . . I appreciate what . . . Head would skin you alive . . . me too, if she caught me . . . there's . . . there's no point to it, I'm afraid . . . we'd never catch him. . . ." She straightened. "No," she said crisply. "I'm back on track, Grey. Forget it." She smiled. "Sometimes it takes a while to get things straight." She fussed with her tumbling hair. "Damn. I swear I'll cut this mess off." She worked two strands loose and used them to knot the rest back from her face. "I'd sell my soul for a comb and some pins."

Chuckling, considerably relieved by her decision, he touched the sensor and sent the skimmer back into the air.

In the yard outside the main building of Chwereva complex, Grey dragged her from the skimmer and plunged through the crowd of watuk. With their adulation and curiosity and excitement nearly suffocating her, she clung to Grey's arm and dived through hands grabbing at her, through a deafening clamor of questions, demands and wild well-wishing.

In the hallway, she gasped with astonishment. "Has that happened before?"

"Sometimes." He grinned at her. "Come on."

In the Rep's office, he went briskly and efficiently through his account of their activities, avoiding problem areas with a casual skill. Aleytys listened with appreciation and admiration.

The Rep's eyes glistened liquidly when Grey described the hare-weapon. Aleytys felt a touch of cold. *All for nothing*, she thought. She glanced at Grey. *Well, no. Hunters Inc. gets its fee and I'm on my way to earning my own ship. And Chwereva will be breeding hares.*

As Grey's ship floated away from Sunguralingu, Aleytys watched the Sawasawa shrink. "I wonder where Manoreh and Kitosime are now, what they're doing." She leaned back and sighed. "Will we ever hear?"

"Probably not." He rested his fingers on the panel of sensor squares. "We could still dogleg to Jaydugar."

"Don't fuss, Grey. I'm fine." She closed her eyes. "There's nothing I can do for my son. I have to accept that." The emptiness was there inside her. "Nothing."

"Lee, come on trek with me when we get back to Wolff."

"What?"

"I need to find my center again." His face and voice were quiet, his eyes were fixed on her. "Too many worlds. Too many Hunts. I've got too far away from something important."

"My center. I wonder if I have one." She swung around and stared at the emptiness filling the viewscreen. "I'll come."

EPILOGUE
Sunguralingu:

The sand was damp and hard under the hooves of the faras. The salt water hissed back and forth in front of the tired, silent line of riders, dirty brown and green up close, edged with foam and a brilliant green-blue where the water met the paler green sky. The smell of dead fish, seaweed and salt was heavy on the brisk wind that snapped at faces and clothes.

"Which way?" Manoreh said.

Faiseh shrugged. "Doesn't matter much. We need to find a fisher hut and get the man to take us out to the islands in his boat." He waved his hand at the horizon. "They're out there but too far from shore to be seen."

Manoreh eased his faras closer to Kitosime. "Kita." He put his hand on her arm.

She was tired, but not too tired to take joy in the warmth that flowed between them. "What is it?"

"Tell us which way. North or south?"

She touched the eyestones in their pouch. After a minute she nodded. "Help me off this creature. If I tried to get down by myself, I'd break my neck."

With a soft laugh he took hold of her waist and lifted her off the faras. Slowly, almost reluctantly, he let her down until her feet were on the sand. Then he slid off his own mount and stood beside her. "What do you need?"

"Fresh water and a little time." She walked apart from the children and sat on the sand. Lifting the pouch cord over her head, she took the stones out and put them on the sand in front of her knees. Manoreh brought her one of the limp waterskins and she squeezed a few drops onto the pale gray stones, filling the eyeholes with darkness. She closed her own eyes and felt the humming of the power blending with the soft brushing of the sea.

172

Flashes of light, small darting sparks of fire . . . A boy's face . . . bright in the darkness . . . the boy from the Tembeat . . . he who had sneaked her in that night . . . the night that began this long trek she'd made from doll to woman . . . he looked down into flames and grieved . . . he led boys over a wall . . . he took a boat . . . loaded the boys in . . . went down a river . . . a wide shiny river . . . reached the coast . . . saw the emptiness of the sea stretching to the horizon . . . and was afraid . . . he sent the boat along the coast . . . stopping at huts . . . stopping again and again in vain . . . the huts were empty . . . then three men came out of the last hut . . . it was close . . . close . . . around a bend . . . no more . . . three men came out of a hut and saw the boat . . . saw it and desired it . . . and fell upon the boys to take it from them . . . happening now . . . right now . . . the boys are fighting . . . struggling . . . right now . . . holding the men off . . . but at what cost . . . three dead already. . . .

She moaned and opened her eyes, stopped the soft mutter of her words. Manoreh and Faiseh were leaning close, listening intently.

Manoreh jumped to his feet. "Umeme!"

Faiseh touched her arm. "Which way, Kitosime? Which way?"

She pointed to the north. "There," she said. "Where the cliffs come close to the sea like a finger poking into the water. On the other side of that."

Faiseh stood beside Manoreh. They exchanged a glance. Then Manoreh reached a hand down to her. She gathered the eyestones, put them back in the pouch, then let him pull her to her feet. "Kita," he said. "Wait a few minutes after we're gone, then bring the children after us. You'll be all right?"

"Am I a doll?"

"Never!" He hugged her quickly then ran to his faras. In minutes he and Faiseh were halfway to the out-thrust of the cliffs.

Kitosime trudged back to her faras, stopped and looked down the line of the children. They were too tired to be curious, just sat passively on their faras, waiting for someone to tell them what to do. She sighed. They needed to stop and rest. She put her hand on the saddle of her faras. "No," she muttered. "I'd rather walk." She took hold of the faras's nose rein and faced the children. "Follow me," she said crisply. She turned and plodded off, looking over her shoulder at intervals to make sure the children were coming after her.

By the time she reached the hut, the fight was over. The bodies of the attackers were stacked like firewood against the wall and the boys were circling excitedly about the two Rangers, all talking at once.

She smiled and began helping the children off their mounts. They staggered a few steps and collapsed to the sand, curling up and going to sleep. Only the older boys kept on their feet and followed her onto the dock. She touched Manoreh's arm. "Is it finished? Are we home?"

He looked out to sea. With a quiet satisfaction, he said, "An hour's sail and we can stop." He fitted her into the curve of his arm. "We can stop and start to build again."

Wolff:

They ran through gray days. Neither spoke beyond what was necessary. They settled into the busy silence of the snow and mist, hearing and not hearing the rhythmic body sounds, the grunts and hoarse breathing, the shish-shish of the snow-shoes.

The first cairn. Aleytys touched the pile of stones but added none of her own. She was not making this trek alone. She smiled at Grey. Already the hard physical labor and the solitude were beginning to work on her. Their eyes met. The smile deepened. They said nothing, but turned and went on.

The silence was deep between them now. A shared silence. Their two solitudes had moved together. In the night camps they were sometimes lovers. It was a good time, a rich time.

The second cairn. They exchanged silent laughter and went on.

Again they were in separate solitudes, turned in on themselves in the grim struggle to maintain sanity as they moved over endless white snow through endless white fog. The air bit now. It was late in winter for a trek. The ice storm came suddenly on them and they were forced into shelter. The days passed, black and dreary. They grated on each other till both were at the point of screaming. They treated each other with an exaggerated courtesy that was by its nature a deadly insult. When the storm passed over and they emerged into the eternal mist, it was almost a time of joy.

The third cairn. They looked grimly at each other and nodded. They went on.

Where Grey had camped on his trek they built two snow shelters and stayed alone, one in each. The nightmares came, the hallucinations and the sudden emergence into clarity.

Grey found his peace again. He watched the yellow lamp flame flicker and wondered if Aleytys had found hers. He sat a long time watching the flame dance over the wick, then he rolled outside and turned to face the other shelter.

Aleytys emerged, springing lightly up onto her feet. She came toward him across the snow like a flame walking, but when she stopped in front of him, her blue-green eyes were filled with tranquility. He reached out. She took his hand. They shared the Wolff-gift while the ghost sun moved slowly past zenith and dipped toward the horizon. Neither spoke. There was no need.